JOHNNY CONCHO

Cripple Creek was Johnny Concho's town. The streets were his, and its people—and its hate.

Johnny never wore a gun, he didn't have to. His brother, Red, was the killer, because he had the fastest draw in the territory.

Then a bullet cut down the legendary Red Concho, and Johnny was left facing Cripple Creek alone, weaponless, and afraid. It simply meant that Johnny Concho had to learn the lessons of manhood in weeks instead of years—that is, if he wanted to live . . .

JOHNNY CONCHO

Noel Loomis and David Harmon

GUNSMOKE

This hardback edition 2002
by Chivers Press
by arrangement with
Golden West Literary Agency

ISBN 0 7540 8204 0

British Library Cataloguing in Publication Data available.

Printed and bound in Great Britain by
BOOKCRAFT, Midsomer Norton, Somerset

JOHNNY CONCHO

Chapter One

This was the best part of the day in Arizona. It was light, but the sun was still below the horizon. The night's coolness had not yet left the land; the air was still and fresh. In the desert to the south the big barrel cacti bloomed in brilliant reds and yellows, while down on the sand, like a carpet, the tiny desert flowers that had sprung up after the rain now tinged the ground with delicate shades of purple, yellow, red, and orange. And somewhere in the distance a nervous road-runner cried *"Chi, chi, chi!"* as it maneuvered to attack a rattlesnake before the reptile found cover from the coming heat.

Johnny Concho, luxuriously waking up in the best bed of the Lang Hotel (which in reality was nothing more than the second floor of the Copper Diggin's Saloon), heard the road-runner's distant chatter and turned over lazily. This was the time of day when he took stock of affairs in Cripple Creek and invariably found himself well satisfied. He was Johnny Concho; he had the best room in the hotel, right at the head of the stairs; he had only to beckon and the entire town of Cripple Creek would run to do his bidding. Now he rolled over again and reminded himself, as he did every morning, that he owed them nothing, really, because it wasn't all going one way. He, Johnny Concho, was giving the townspeople value received.

The road-runner's cry came again, and then the approaching clop of horses' hoofs and Johnny Concho, abruptly wide awake, swung to a sitting position on the side of his bed and from his window scrutinized, with some concern, Cripple Creek's one and only street.

It was like any main street in Arizona in the 1890's—wide, trailing off at the south into a desert of cacti, disappearing at the north in the direction of a distant mountain range. The street's surface was rutted and its dirt ground flour-fine by the shod hoofs of horses, the smaller shoes of mules, and the splayed feet of oxen; by the narrow iron tires of buggies, the huge four-inch-wide tires of freight wagons headed for the copper mines in the distant mountains.

The buildings along the street were flimsy, most of them unpainted except for the wide false fronts. Albert Dark's general store had a wooden sidewalk, for Dark had been a Boston man before he came West for his health. The bakery, the pharmacy—most of them were not as pretentious. Most of Cripple Creek's inhabitants were content to let things take their course, and each one unwilling, Johnny thought somewhat sardonically, to fight his own battles, to risk any small portion of his own comfort—which made it all the better for Johnny Concho.

On both sides of the street, and backing it up in very scattered and haphazard fashion, were a few houses that held most of Cripple Creek's one hundred and ninety inhabitants. And Johnny, looking for the source of the hoofbeats, observed that smoke was already coming from the chimney of Joe Helgeson's blacksmith shop, and presently the rhythmical clang of big Helgeson's hammer on hot iron would awaken the town to another day.

But Johnny still didn't place the steady hoofbeats. He sat up straight on the edge of the bed and pulled the worn lace curtain a little wider. He saw a long funnel of dust, slow to settle in the quiet air, and two men coming in from the east. He stared at them for a moment, wondering where two strangers would come from at such an early hour. Their horses looked fresh, so they must have camped during the night. Why hadn't they come on into town instead?

Obviously this was a situation that called for Johnny's unusual talents to be brought into play. He got to his feet, yawned, went to the chair and put on his brown wool pants and checkered shirt, pulled his soft, wide-brimmed hat from a nail in the wall, considered combing his hair but decided against it. He pulled on his hat and went out. He wore no gun; he did not, in fact, own a pistol of any kind.

He went down the stairway with no effort to be quiet. He walked loudly across the bare boards of the hotel floor, and went outside.

The two riders were just pulling up to the hitch-rail in front of the post office. One, a little in advance, wore battered levis and a faded blue shirt; he carried two six-shooters. The second was taller, with sharp eyes and a hard jaw; he was dressed in black, and he also wore two six-shooters.

Johnny stepped forward and said pleasantly, "Mornin', gents."

The one in advance said, "Howdy." The one behind said nothing.

"Somethin'?" asked Johnny.

"Just lookin'," said the man in the blue shirt.

"Couple of two-gun men," said Johnny. "Come from Tombstone, maybe?"

"We didn't say."

"Maybe," said Johnny, still pleasant, "you was left over from the fight in the OK Corral, or maybe you resigned from the Graham-Tewkesbury feud."

"We—"

"Shut up, Walker!" the second man said harshly. "We didn't come here to be questioned by no two-bit gambler."

Johnny was enjoying this. It was always interesting to watch them crawfish when they found out who he was. "I don't gamble for a living," he said.

"Wait a minute, Tallman," said Walker. "Has he got a star on him?"

"No star," said Tallman, "and no iron to back up a star *or* his words."

Walker said easily, "We come to look the town over, sonny."

"We're thinkin' pretty strong of settlin' down," said Tallman. "We been movin' around too much."

"All we need," Walker added, "is to find the right town."

Johnny said, shaking his head: "This isn't the right town, boys. Move on."

They both stared at him. Tallman's right hand moved

toward his pistol, but Walker held up a warning hand. "Wait a minute, Tallman. Be careful. This may be a trap."

"In a way," Johnny said, "you might call it that. This town is Cripple Creek, and I'm Johnny Concho. It's my town."

Walker looked steadily down at him. Tallman squinted. "Johnny Concho? Never heard of you, mister—and we ain't in no humor to be bluffed by a pair that couldn't even open."

Johnny yawned. "You heard of Red Concho?"

Tallman didn't answer for a minute. Finally he said, "We might of."

Johnny nodded. "It's for sure you never got closer than that." His voice suddenly turned cold, for this was the kill. "You're a couple of tinhorn gunslingers, and neither one of you is man enough to lay a finger on Red Concho's back-trail—and you know it. Red Concho cleaned out Tombstone. Red Concho shot up Bisbee. Red Concho made Yuma dance the jig. And Red Concho is my brother."

He watched them to see the effects of this announcement.

Walker continued to stare at him. Tallman moistened his lips a little. "Your brother, eh?" He considered this. "So you're layin' tribute on Cripple Creek in the name of Red Concho, eh? Without no guns, without no fightin', without no risk. You just say 'Red Concho' and everybody is supposed to git. And you ain't even a marshal!"

"There's no need to be," said Johnny Concho.

Tallman's head seemed to sink a little between his big shoulders. "Maybe not, mister, maybe not. But what would happen to you and your little town if something happened to your brother?"

Johnny straightened. "The man don't live that can gun Red!"

Tallman seemed thoughtful. "They said that about Jesse James—but they were wrong."

"When they say it about Red, they're right! Remember this, mister, if you get any ideas: Red is the fastest man on the draw and the straightest shot in Arizona."

"So far."

"That's far enough."

"If he's so good," said Tallman, "why does he still use that bullwhip?"

"He's good enough," said Johnny, "that he doesn't have to use his guns very often."

"Or is it," said Tallman, "that he just likes to lay open the meat on a man's back?"

Johnny said harshly, "I told you once to get out of town—and stay out!"

Tallman's eyes narrowed as he watched Johnny. Finally he raised his left hand and slapped his horse's withers with the ends of the reins. "Maybe you'll see us back in Cripple Creek," he said as the horse moved on.

Johnny stood for a moment, watching them leave by the south road. Then he quelled the tightness that had come over him at mention of Red. He turned slowly.

Men and women were watching him from doors along the street, seemingly sprung up out of nowhere, the way they always did when something was going on. You could have snapped off a rattlesnake's head in the middle of the night, and half a minute later every door along the street would be filled with inquisitive but cautious faces.

Pete Henderson, the sheriff, was standing just outside his office, watching. Up at the end of the street Joe Helgeson filled the door of his blacksmith shop. Bennie, the bachelor restaurant man, was outside on the street, probably not able to see too well because of his poor eyesight, but trying to understand what had happened. Judge Earl Tyler, showing an overimpassive face for a man under forty, watched through the small window of his office. Old Josh, the alcohol-soaked swamper at the Copper Diggin's, was coming from Mrs. Brown's, where he had a room, and he said hastily, "Mornin', Mister Concho."

Johnny didn't look at him, and didn't answer.

Albert Dark, a mild little man in a derby hat, had come outside to sweep the board sidewalk. "Mornin', Mr. Concho," he said with a quick smile.

Johnny glanced at him from under half-closed lids, but didn't answer.

Duke Lang and his wife Pearl had come down the stairs behind Johnny. Duke must have dressed pretty fast, but he was wearing his flashy brocaded vest, and his heavy blond mustache was carefully twisted at the ends. Johnny saw them, nodded briefly at Duke, and said to Pearl, "Had breakfast?"

She smiled. "Not yet. We just got up."

"Eat with me?" said Johnny.

She smiled. "Sure, Johnny."

"You?" Johnny asked Duke.

"Nope. Got to open up."

That was the way it always was, and Johnny was glad. He had no wish to eat breakfast with Duke Lang. Likewise, Duke never offered any interference to Pearl's eating with Johnny. It seemed a little strange that a man wouldn't keep a closer eye on his wife, but then Pearl had a mind of her own, and it seemed to be part of her job to be pleasant to men who came into the saloon, so Johnny guessed there was nothing unusual about it.

In some towns Duke Lang would have run the town—and probably in Cripple Creek too, if Johnny hadn't been the younger brother of Red Concho.

Pearl stepped down and took Johnny's arm. She had a nice dress of some kind of rustly silk—Pearl never wore gingham or calico—that was light blue with a white collar. They walked up the street and went into Bennie's, and Bennie rubbed his hands. "What'll it be this morning, Mr. Concho?"

"Ham and eggs, I guess. What else is there?"

"Beefsteak. Pie. There's still some of the doughnuts I made last week. You said you liked them, Mr. Concho."

"Ham and eggs," said Johnny. "What'll you have, Pearl?"

"Coffee, Johnny."

"No pie?"

"It fills me out too much," she said.

Johnny guessed that if she filled out much more she'd bust a martingale on the blue dress, but he didn't say so.

Bennie went to work at the stove, and in a minute the sound of sizzling meat filled the little room.

"Pearl," said Johnny, "you like it here?"

She looked at him sidewise. "It's a living."

He liked her voice, low and a little husky and aimed at him. "I've seen better," she said. "In Phoenix there was money, and nice dresses, and men who weren't afraid to spend."

He noticed her moodiness. "You miss that?"

"A lot—sometimes." She looked up. "Do you like it here, Johnny?"

He shrugged. "Never really lived anywhere else since I was a kid."

"That hasn't been very long," she observed.

Bennie set a big white crockery platter in front of Johnny. "Coffee coming up," he said brightly.

"Sometimes I can't stand it here," said Pearl. "It's a small town—" her voice was scornful— "and everybody watches you every minute."

"What's wrong with that?"

She studied him carefully. "Nothin'—only I feel like cuttin' loose once in a while—but here you don't dare."

Johnny didn't quite understand the significance of her words, but he didn't worry about it. He finished his breakfast and said to Bennie, "Charge it," and Bennie said, "Yes, sir, Mr. Concho."

Then Johnny asked Pearl, "Sure you won't have a piece of pie?"

"No, thanks, Johnny."

He nodded. They separated at the door, and Johnny went to the blacksmith shop. Joe Helgeson, a huge man wearing a leather apron, but bare from the waist up, and hairy-chested, was pulling a red-hot wagon iron from the fire with a pair of tongs. Helgeson didn't look up.

Johnny stopped. Sometimes Helgeson annoyed him, for although Helgeson did all the things Johnny required, sometimes he showed resentment. "You shoe my horse, Helgeson?" asked Johnny.

Helgeson nodded, still without looking up. "Stabled in the back."

Johnny smiled a little. Helgeson was a stubborn Scandinavian; he knew as well as anybody Johnny's value to a town like Cripple Creek, but he'd never admit it.

Johnny went through the blacksmith shop and opened the gate to the stable. Along one side there were five stalls—three occupied, two empty. On the other side were a light buggy and a spring wagon. Johnny went to the third stall and scrutinized the big black horse munching oats. The horse, switching flies with its tail, caught sight of him and turned its head. Johnny looked at its shoes.

The horse tried to turn around in the stall, but the halter rope jerked its head. Johnny went back into the blacksmith shop.

"You polish my saddle?" he asked Helgeson.

The blacksmith nodded toward the wall near the front door. Johnny went closer. A saddle hung on a two-by-four at the right side of the door. He went up to it and looked it over. It was a little worn, but a nice saddle, well decorated with heavy silver *conchas*. Johnny punched the leather with his fingertips. "The next time," he said, "use some saddlesoap. The leather's drying out."

Helgeson shrugged. "You don't need to be so finicky. You'll strike matches on it anyway. And matches leave marks."

"You know I don't strike matches on a good saddle." He added softly, "The next time, use saddlesoap."

"All right," Helgeson said grudgingly.

Johnny looked across the doorway at the saddle hanging on the opposite side, and then at Helgeson. This was a little ritual that Johnny secretly enjoyed. Helgeson, trying to make it seem that he was looking at the iron, was really watching Johnny, and his sullenness had given way to apprehension.

The saddle was made out of fine tooled leather and decorated profusely with gold filigree; the *conchas* and the plate on top of the saddlehorn and the rim of the cantle all were gold that gleamed in the leaping light of the forge fire. Johnny touched the gold-rimmed cantle; he ran his hand down the stirrup strap; he took hold of the saddlehorn and partially lifted the saddle, to hear the pleasant creak of new leather. He turned back to Helgeson, who, scowling, was thrusting the wagon iron back into the fire.

"Beautiful saddle," said Johnny.

Helgeson grunted.

"Saw one like that in Holbrook once. Sort of an exhibition. They said it was worth fifteen hundred dollars."

Helgeson's lips were tight in the red light of the fire as he worked the bellows that made the fire turn blue.

"A man would be proud to have a saddle like that—all that gold."

"The gold is nothing," Helgeson said gruffly. "It is the work that goes into it—the work of a man's hands—

the shaping, the fitting. Those are things that make a saddle."

"This one has all that," Johnny said. "You can see it."

Helgeson said, "You know how many months I worked shaping that fork and fitting and tooling that leather? You know how many horses I shoed and how many wagon tires I fitted to pay for that gold?" He hitched up his leather apron. "I sweat blood to build that saddle."

"You still say it isn't for sale?"

"I still say it."

Johnny nodded. "I'll wait." He went over to his own saddle, took it by the horn, slid it off of the two-by-four, dropped it on the ground at Helgeson's feet, and said, "Saddle up the black and walk him to the sheriff's office in a couple of hours."

He watched Helgeson for a moment. The big man's face tightened. He hit the iron harder but he didn't look at Johnny. He turned the iron over, and Johnny left him and walked out of the shop.

Chapter Two

Albert Dark had gone back inside his store, and Johnny opened the door and went in. He tried to close his nostrils against the odor of horse tonic and stock medicine, kerosene and turpentine.

Albert Dark, still wearing his derby, was showing Mrs. Brown, a sharp-featured woman whose husband was a freighter on the run to Flagstaff, a new alarm clock. "It's very simple, Mrs. Brown. You just pull this lever forward and it will ring whenever it says on this small dial; then—"

Johnny turned away. He couldn't see why Mrs. Brown needed an alarm clock; she had her nose in everybody's business most of the time anyway. No wonder, thought Johnny, her husband stayed away from home most of the time. He looked at the glass case with lemon drops and hoarhound and a box full of thin cocoanut candy with colored flags in the center. Behind the candy case, on the shelves, were rows of patent medicines—Tutt's Liver Pills, Hood's Sarsaparilla, Piso's Consumption Cure (that was one of Albert Dark's favorites, for he had used it himself), Carbolate of Tar Inhalant, Dr. Kline's Great Nerve Restorer, and Dr. Haines's Golden Specific for curing drunkenness. Next to the medicines were bolts of goods—mostly calicos and ginghams, and then a pile of blankets. Toward the back were bridles and a set of harness, horse collars, pitchforks. Up the other side were foods—beans, dried fruits in small barrels, a hogshead of pickles, an opened wooden box of crackers, a round of cheese with several slices missing. Up near the front were two rifles on nails, a pair of double-action Colts, and a shelf filled with boxes of ammunition.

Johnny stopped at the cheese. A long-bladed knife was stuck point-down in the board, and Johnny plucked it up easily, balanced it in his hand, and cut a thick pie-shaped wedge of cheese. He got a handful of crackers out of the barrel and arranged them on each side of the wedge. He surveyed this, then put the cheese on the board and sliced it through the middle. He went to the sweet-pickle barrel and fished in it with the long fork until he had three

14

pickles, which he sliced in half and placed between the halves of cheese. Then he rearranged the crackers on the outside, looked it over, liked what he saw, and took a huge bite out of the thin edge, watching Albert Dark demonstrate the clock.

"It's got a guarantee, Mrs. Brown," said Dark.

"The last one had a guarantee," she answered sharply.

"If you aren't satisfied at any time, the company will be glad to refund your money."

"I wasn't satisfied the last time," said Mrs. Brown, "but I didn't get my money back."

"They gave you a new one. Remember?"

"It's not the same thing," she said, and took the package. She gave him a small gold coin, and he pulled a wallet out of his pocket and made change. She counted it twice, then put it into her purse.

Johnny was sitting on the counter, munching his cheese sandwich. Mrs. Brown glared at him. "I declare!" she said. "Some people have more nerve!" She swept out of the store.

"And some people have less," said Johnny tolerantly.

Albert Dark watched her leave, shaking his head. "Some day," he said, "I'm going back to Boston and open a store for ladies and gentlemen. Real ladies who walk like ladies and talk like ladies." He sighed. "Morning, Mr. Concho."

"Got those things I ordered?" asked Johnny.

"Yes, sir. Got everything. Set them aside for you and wrapped them up." He turned and took a package from the shelf behind him. "Razor strop, shaving soap, two shirts size fifteen, a belt like the one I got for Duke Lang, but fancier—" He finished turning around and pushed the package across the counter. "Ought to have good weather for the next few weeks."

"Good weather for riding," said Johnny, thinking of Walker and Tallman.

"I'd like to be ridin' somewhere—anywhere. When I came out here from Boston, one of the first things I was going to do was ride a horse. And do you know, Mr. Concho, that was fifteen years ago and I ain't rode a horse yet."

"That reminds me," said Johnny, "I need a horse blanket."

"Horse blanket? Yes, sir." Albert Dark turned back to the shelves, but his movements were puttery. "Horse blanket . . . horse blanket." Suddenly he turned to Johnny, his eyes shining. He leaned across the counter and whispered hoarsely, "I saw what happened this morning, Mr. Concho. I saw you run those two badmen out of town."

Johnny felt pleased. "You liked it?"

"It has been the ambition of my life," said Albert Dark, "to run a badman out of town the way you did."

Johnny grinned lazily.

"I never even fired a pistol," said Dark. "I've tried." He held his right hand at arm's length and turned his head away. "I can't even pull the trigger. My hand isn't steady. I'm afraid I'll hit the wrong thing."

Johnny said, "Try both hands next time."

"Both hands?" Dark stared at him for a second. "Both hands?" He seemed to be trying to visualize it.

"The blanket," Johnny said impatiently.

"Yes, sir, the blanket." Dark turned back aimlessly. "Wife is always rearranging things. What is it that drives a woman to—"

Johnny said sharply, "The blanket!"

"Oh—of course." He went to a shelf near the bolt goods, and returned with two blankets, which he spread out on the counter. "Now this one—this one is two and a half, but this one—this is an extra-fine blanket, Navajo weave. Costs four dollars. You won't find a finer horse blanket in the West."

A curtain moved behind him, and a plain-faced woman, her gray hair pulled straight back and twisted into a knot on her neck, came out, glanced at Albert and Johnny, and went to Albert's side. She pushed the cheaper blanket at Johnny. "This one's good enough for a horse," she said.

Johnny smiled. "Not my horse, ma'am."

She bristled. "I know your horse. I knew it when it belonged to Sam Green."

Johnny said, "A mighty good horse. That's why I bought it."

She said pointedly, "Buyin' and payin' is two different things."

Albert raised his hands. "Now, Sarah—"

Johnny felt the two-fifty blanket and the four-dollar

blanket. "A good horse needs a good blanket," he said. "I'll take this one. Just add it to my bill."

"Yes, sir, Mr. Concho."

Sarah said with heavy sarcasm, *"Mister* Concho."

Albert sounded scared. "Sarah—"

Johnny rolled up the blanket and laid it across his package, then faced Sarah Dark. "Mrs. Dark, I don't think I like you," he said, still talking pleasantly.

Sarah said belligerently, "Mr. Concho, I don't think I care."

Johnny smiled slowly. "Where's Mary?" he asked.

"You stay away from Mary!"

Johnny looked at Albert. "Where is she?"

"In the kitchen, Mr. Concho."

"Thanks."

Sarah moved to stop him, but Johnny was around the end of the counter and through the curtain before she could get in his way. He reached the curtain and turned to look at her. Sarah was glaring at Albert. "You coward!" she said.

Johnny called back, "Albert, your wife talks strong language for a woman."

Albert Dark, obviously embarrassed, looked first at Johnny and then at his wife. "Sarah, hold your tongue!"

She glared at him and then at Johnny, and Johnny knew what was eating her: that Johnny had such a hold that he had forced her own husband to reprimand her in public.

The kitchen was filled with the soft, warm smell of fresh bread, and Johnny stopped, making no sound. Mary had just slid a pan of new loaves into the oven. "Hello, Johnny," she said before she looked around, and arose to close the oven door.

He stepped inside. "How did you know I was here?"

She turned toward him with a smile. Her hair was black and glossy and she didn't pull it straight back like her mother's, but allowed it to fluff up around her head. "I always know when you're near me, Johnny."

They looked at each other. Her eyes were warm and soft, and Johnny began to melt a little inside.

She turned and hung the padded cloth on the rod at the front of the stove.

"What are you baking?" Johnny asked, to be saying something.

"Nothing fancy, Johnny. Just light-bread."

"Kitchen smells always remind me of home—when Red and I were kids."

"It's hard to imagine Red Concho as a kid," she said.

"Why?"

"I don't know. It's just that I always picture him as—" She hesitated.

"A gunhand?"

She looked at him. "It's not something I like to say to you, Johnny, but that's the way I picture him. You told me he used to sit around cleaning a pistol when the other kids were out playing." She shuddered.

Johnny said, "When the other kids were running around at night, playing run-sheep-run, Red was home, practicing his draw in front of a looking-glass."

"And you, Johnny—did you practice drawing?"

His eyes were wide. "I didn't need to. I had Red."

But she was unexpectedly sober. "He's been no good for you, Johnny."

"You're wrong about Red, Mary. He was a good kid— and smart too. He went all the way to the seventh grade."

"He must have been brilliant."

Johnny ignored her sarcasm. "He would have kept on, only—"

"Only what?"

"They asked him to leave. One of the teachers got out of hand and hit Red, made him mad." He paused. "He never hit Red again."

Mary asked, "What did your brother do to the teacher?"

"I don't think you'd like to hear about it."

Mary said heavily, "I don't think I'd like to hear *anything* about Red Concho."

She went to the oven and looked in, careful not to jar the stove. She reached for the padded cloth and bent down and pulled out the upper pan of bread. She tapped the crust. She wet her finger and snapped it on the bottom of the pan. It sizzled. She took the pan in both hands to the table, turned it over, shook the six loaves loose, and put the empty pan on the water reservoir at the end of the stove. Johnny watched carefully. Her face was flushed from the heat, but there was a look of strain about it too. He watched her drape the padded cloth over the shiny rod, and said, "You hate him, don't you, Mary?"

"Yes," she admitted. "I hate him."

Johnny frowned. "He's never hurt you," he said.

"If you mean he's never gunned me or cut me with his bullwhip, you're right—but he's ruined you, Johnny, and that hurts me."

He walked across the room, then turned to stare at her. "Mary, you never really knew anything about Red and me when we were kids, did you?"

"No."

"We were raised in a little town in New Mexico Territory, and our mother died when we were little. Then we moved near Tucson, and my dad was foreman on a ranch. But he was shot by a cattle rustler—shot in the back, Mary!"

She walked to the table and looked at the bread without seeing it. Then she looked up at him, her eyes misty.

"That's when Red was in the seventh grade," said Johnny. "He went out and got the rustler, and the teacher tried to give him a whipping for being out of school without an excuse. Whip Red Concho!"

"Yes, Johnny?"

"Red was thirteen; I was ten—and after that we moved. Red took care of me. He was all the family I had after that. Don't you see, Mary? He looked out for me, he saw that I got food and clothing. Sometimes it wasn't much, but Red would always say, 'Don't worry, kid. We'll see better days.' Mary, don't you understand?"

She reached out her hand toward him, and he took her in his arms. "Oh, Johnny!" she cried. "I'm sorry about your—your folks, and I'm glad Red took care of you, but—"

"But what?"

"If only it had been different!" she whispered. "He's done something to you, Johnny."

He considered this. "You don't like the way I am," he observed, "but you *love* me."

She turned, tears in her eyes, and reached for a clean dish towel. Her fingers fumbled, but she picked up the towel and placed it over the fresh loaves of bread.

He was at a loss for a moment. Then he said with bravado, "Don't worry about the Concho brothers, Mary. They're gonna do just fine."

He started to leave. She was still putting the cloth in place around the bread, but she looked up and called, "Johnny!"

He stopped and faced her.

"Look in the mirror, Johnny. You're not a schoolboy any more. Look in the mirror and see yourself for what you are."

He exploded. "What do you want me to see, Mary?" His voice was hard. "A man made out of nothing—raised by an older brother who wasn't afraid to fight for him. Is that what you want me to see: just that part, not the part where two kids came up from nothing, not the part where no man in Arizona will stand up to Red Concho's guns? Is that what you want me to see?" His words were harsh. "Is that what you see, and what all the rest see?" He took her by the shoulders. "I see more, Mary. Red put me here in Cripple Creek to do a job. He said there was nobody in Cripple Creek who had the guts to keep the badmen away, and he told me to stay here and do it for them, and he would back me up. I've done that—with Red behind me. What more can you ask, Mary? I'm the only one in town who isn't afraid. Does that make me a schoolboy?"

Her head was turned away, and she didn't answer. Johnny released her roughly, and she almost fell. Then he turned quickly from her, strode back and yanked the curtain aside. He paused and glared at Sarah and Albert Dark, who looked frightened. He snatched up his package from the counter, picked up the rolled blanket, dropped it on the floor, picked it up again, then got outside.

He was breathing fast, walking with hard, angry steps. Why couldn't Mary stop worrying him about Red, making him uncertain, trying to make him feel little? Every time they saw each other they argued about Red. And she was wrong. If he had any sense he'd quit going around to see her. But the thought of not seeing Mary took something out from under him, because she loved him, and he knew it was something a man could count on. Her eyes glowed softly when she looked at him, and her pink lips were his alone. She was pretty, and more—Mary was the only one in Cripple Creek who really smiled at him from inside.

He wouldn't quit her. He'd show her she was wrong.

He was breathing more easily as he reached the end of the second block. It was mid-morning now, and heat lay in heavy layers the length of main street. Again the town seemed deserted except for a burro browsing on a few blades of grama grass back of the bakery.

Johnny stopped at a sign that said, *Real Estate. U. S. Land Commissioner* on the window. He walked in. The outer office was empty, and he turned to the left, into a small room with a desk, two chairs, a bulletin board covered with "wanted" posters, and a rack of rifles on the wall.

Pete Henderson was a portly man who wore his hat pushed back on his head like a man who had nothing to fear and nothing to hide. A somewhat tarnished star was pinned to his left shirt front, but his gunbelt, with a gun in the holster, was hanging on a nail beside the door. Pete was about sixty, portly and easygoing. "Hello, Johnny," he said.

Johnny sat down. "Somebody said you wanted to see me, Sheriff."

"That's right."

"What's on your mind?"

"I've got a little advice for you."

"I don't remember asking for it," said Johnny.

"You better listen anyway." Henderson got up, looked through the door into the outer office, and came back to stand in front of Johnny. "You're pushin' Cripple Creek too hard, Johnny."

"I am?"

"Yes. It's bad for everybody in a town to hate you."

"Everybody?" asked Johnny.

Henderson nodded. "I'm afraid so."

Johnny put his feet up on the desk and leaned back. "How about you, Sheriff? Do you hate Johnny Concho?"

"I go with the pack, son."

"So I've noticed," said Johnny.

"I'm talkin' for your own good, Johnny."

"You never answered my question. Do *you* hate me, Sheriff?"

"No, I can't say as I do, really. You ain't done much to make me like you, but that ain't the same as hatin'."

Johnny sat up straight. "All right. Mary Dark doesn't hate me, and I don't think her father hates me. That makes three who don't hate me that I can name right off."

Henderson grunted.

Johnny went on, "I don't think these people hate me as much as you say they do or even as much as they think they do. Sure, they growl about it, but they know who's takin' care of Cripple Creek. They know Red watches over Cripple Creek because I'm here, and they'd be the first to holler if anything happened to me or Red. So would you, Sheriff."

"Me?"

"Sure. How many times have you had those guns on in the last two years?"

"Not many," the sheriff admitted.

"Not once that I can remember. Why?"

"Well—"

"I'll tell you why," said Johnny. "Because you've got Red's guns behind you—and you know it. When Red told me to watch things for him, he said it so loud everybody in Arizona could hear it. And don't you think they know what that means?"

The sheriff rubbed his jaw. "The people—"

"The people don't really hate me *or* Red. If I thought they did I'd—"

"You keep shovin' people around, there's gonna be a noise."

"Did I ever shoot anybody or beat anybody up or use a knife on anybody?"

"Can't say you have—but there's other ways to push people around. . . . I don't want any trouble, Johnny."

Johnny stood up. He wasn't any taller than the sheriff, but his voice was hard. "Then stay off my back—you and the rest of the town. Whether you like it or not, I'm running things in Cripple Creek, and if you and your friends don't like it, move on."

"You talk awful hard, son."

"I've got a big whip." Johnny turned to the door and then looked back. "I'll tell you something else, Henderson. Red told it to me. He said one man can run any town as long as there isn't anybody in that town got guts enough to stick his own neck out, to make the town act together." His voice was filled with scorn. "And you know damned well that will never happen in Cripple Creek."

Henderson took a deep breath. "Red Concho has got Cripple Creek under his thumb," he admitted. "But what will happen when your brother isn't around any longer?"

Johnny said sharply, "That ain't gonna happen—ever! The man don't live that—wait a minute, you're the second one said that today."

Henderson raised his eyebrows. "Might be worth thinkin' about, Johnny."

Johnny's eyes were narrow. "You through with your advice, old man?"

"I'm through."

"Okay. Now get busy and earn your money. I'm goin' out to meet the stage from Holbrook."

"Lookin' for mail?"

"I'm looking for a letter from Red."

Henderson frowned. "Johnny, it ain't good—your lookin' up to Red like that."

"I didn't ask your opinion."

"Some day you'll have to stand on your own two feet, and—"

"You said that once!" Johnny's voice snapped. "Now get out and pass the word around: I want to play poker tonight. Tell my friends to be there—including those who hate me!"

He went outside. Helgeson plodded up, leading the black. Johnny stepped forward, snatched the reins, and mounted. He paid no attention to Helgeson's sullen face. He saw Albert Dark and his wife watching him from their door, but he looked for Mary, and was satisfied when he saw her dark head in the window. He nodded to her and saw her wave. He raised in the stirrups and turned in the saddle, one hand on the cantle; the sheriff was in the doorway, watching him leave. Duke Lang and Pearl stood in the doorway of the Copper Diggin's. Johnny ignored them all. He let the black trot up the street. Then he kicked it into a lope; he left the road and started across the hard, sun-baked ground toward the distant mountains.

Chapter Three

HE STOPPED the black by a tall soapweed on the crest of a hill to give it a breather. From there he could see the town of Cripple Creek, the road winding in and out of town and lost on the desert. To the east he saw a cloud of dust, and watched until it came closer and he could identify the six-mule team of the stagecoach. He kicked the horse and went down the slope at a hard gallop.

He saw the driver look his way and then tap the shotgun messenger on the arm. That man brought his Winchester up into his arms, cradled, and kept his eyes on Johnny.

Johnny rode alongside. "You're late!" he shouted. "Pull 'em down!"

The driver braced his feet and pulled back on the six lines and threw mule talk at the team. They came to a stop. "This ain't gonna make us get there any faster," he said grumpily.

A big man with a shock of white hair stuck his head out of the window. "Any trouble up there?" he asked.

"No trouble," said the driver, and the white-haired man pulled his head back inside.

"Know who that was?" the driver asked Johnny.

"Nope."

"Reverend Barney Clark."

Johnny refused to be impressed. "Never heard of him."

"Fastest gunslinger in Arizona Territory."

Johnny looked up. "Him? He's a has-been."

"He's lived a long time. Was marshal of El Paso after Stoudenmier was killed; marshal of Tombstone three years. And they say he put more men in boothill than all the gunslingers in Cochise County."

"What's he doing here?" asked Johnny quickly.

"Turned to savin' souls instead of shootin' killers. He claims there's no power in a gun anyway; the power is in the man behind it."

"Some day," said Johnny, "I'll go listen to his sermons. Have you got a letter for me?"

The driver shook his head. "They never gave me one at Holbrook."

"There ought to be a letter from Red," said Johnny.

"I'm sorry, Mr. Concho. Not this time."

"Maybe," said Johnny, "it's in the mailbag."

"Nobody said nothin' about it."

"Let's have a look," said Johnny. "Pull the mailbag out of the boot there."

"Can't do it."

Johnny insisted. "I want that letter."

"Listen, Johnny. That mailbag is locked. I can't give you a piece of mail out of there. I have to deliver it to the postmaster."

"Locked?" asked Johnny. "You've got a knife, Milo, haven't you? Cut it open."

"Look, Johnny," said Milo. "This isn't like when I'm carryin' a letter in my hat for you. This is different. You're violatin' a federal law if you touch that mailbag."

"Federal law?" Johnny snorted. "Never heard of it. We got a judge and a sheriff in Cripple Creek, but they don't represent the federal law. Anyway, nobody is coming after me for taking a letter addressed to me."

"Johnny, I'm tellin' you: it's serious, touchin' that mailbag."

"I'm not afraid to slice the whole damn' thing up," said Johnny.

"They'll put your picture on a poster as a holdup man—"

Johnny frowned. "Nobody has ever called a Concho a holdup man. All right!" he shouted. "Get moving!" He slapped the wheel-horse on the rump with the ends of his reins and let out a wild cry: "Heieiii!"

The horses bolted forward. For a moment it looked as if the wheel-horses would run over the lead span and the swing span, but they all broke into a gallop and the coach lurched into motion with a creaking of leather and wood. The driver and the shotgun man grabbed the seat irons to hold on. Johnny grinned. He turned the black and trotted back to the north. There was a piece of land up there that he might buy, so that Red would have a place to settle when he got tired of roaming. That was one reason Johnny had wanted that letter. He had talked to Red about the land,

and Red had said he would send him some mining options that he could sell for enough to buy the property. One option in particular, Red had said, was worth a good deal of money, and Red had suggested Johnny buy the land in his own name and hang onto it.

Johnny rode on north for a couple of hours and made a circuit of the land. There were a couple of sections, and the sage was not high, but thick and bushy, indicating moisture. The grass was much better than it was to the south of town, and there was no cactus up here. Along the northern edge was a small creek that never went dry, for along it were willows and old cottonwoods. A heavy growth of young stuff only would have meant water one year and a dry stream the next; but for miles, east to west, there was this fringe of bright green with an occasional old patriarch towering above the rest and loaded with green leaves. It looked good. As soon as he got the options he would take a sashay into Silver City and turn them into money. Then this land would be his and Red's. They would buy some feeding steers and settle down to ranch life. Red wouldn't have to depend on his guns any longer.

Johnny rode into Cripple Creek about dark and took his horse to the stable. Helgeson was not there, and Johnny smiled, knowing the big Scandinavian would be waiting at the saloon, fuming and impatient. He took his time unsaddling, rubbing down the horse, giving it some oats. Then he walked down the street to the Copper Diggin's.

Pearl was sitting at a small round table talking to a rancher; a bottle of whisky was on the table before them, but Pearl wasn't drinking. She was wearing a wine-colored taffeta dress that was kind to her face, and her arms were bare; she had nice arms. Duke, in his fancy vest and his waxed mustaches, stood at the bar between two men in batwing collars and Prince Albert coats. They were Easterners but they both were big men and looked well able to take care of themselves.

At a table on the left sat Joe Helgeson, Albert Dark, and two other men, Sam Green and Judge Earl Tyler. One chair was empty. Each man had a stack of chips in front of him, and there was a deck of cards in the center of the table, but the men were not playing.

Sam Green was a tough little rancher who walked hard to show people that he couldn't be pushed around. He saw Johnny and said, "You're takin' your own sweet time."

Albert Dark said meekly, "I'm in no hurry, Sam."

Sam said fiercely, "Well, I am. My ranch won't run itself. I've got three hundred head of steers waitin' for the dipping vat."

Judge Tyler said soothingly, "Johnny will be down in a minute. Won't you, Johnny?"

"What time is it, Judge?" Sam Green asked.

"It's—oh, I forgot. My watch—"

Johnny watched him flounder. Then Johnny pulled Tyler's gold watch out of his own vest pocket and studied it leisurely. The judge looked pained as he glanced at the watch. "I shouldn't ever have put it up for stakes," he said. "That was my father's watch and chain."

"It's three minutes after eight," said Johnny, and put the watch back in his pocket.

One of the Easterners asked, "Think the stage to Silver City will pull out on time?"

The other man said, "I heard the postmaster say he might hold over tonight if he got in late."

Duke said, "He's done that before. Drink up, gents. The next one's on the house."

"I'm Pearson," said the first man. "My partner's Benson. We deal in mining options."

Benson choked. "You must get your whisky from Kentucky," he said.

Duke snorted. "Hundred-proof alkali. Made right up here in the hills."

"Do you think," asked Pearson, "they'd mind if we sat in on the game?"

Johnny allowed a fleeting smile to cross his face. Duke saw it, and said to Pearson, "It's a private game."

Johnny went upstairs. He took his time washing, and put on his new fawn-colored pants, a flowered vest with the heavy watch chain conspicuous across the front of it, and a black coat. Then he went down the stairs, stopped on the bottom step, looked around at them all, smiled, and went to the poker table.

"Harry," Duke called to the bartender, "take Mr. Concho a stack of chips."

"Yes, sir," said Harry. "Will a hundred be enough?"
"More than enough," Duke said sourly.

Johnny sat down. He heard Pearson say, "Isn't that the man who met the stagecoach this morning?"

"Sure," said Duke. "That's Johnny Concho."

"Concho? Any kin to Red Concho over around Holbrook?"

"Younger brother," said Duke.

Johnny was conscious that Pearson was staring at him. "I think I'll watch the game," said Pearson, and he said to the bartender, "I've got a bad taste in my mouth."

"So have I," Duke said, and turned back to the bar. "Give me another shot."

"Your deal, Judge," said Johnny.

Judge Tyler picked up the deck, shuffled, pushed the deck over to Johnny for the cut, picked up the two stacks, put them together, and dealt, one card at a time.

"You gentlemen mind if I watch?" asked Pearson.

Albert Dark said, "We don't mind." He looked around the table. "Do we?"

There was no answer, and Pearson took a place behind Johnny.

Helgeson looked at his cards and laid them face down again. "Open for five." He tossed in a chip.

Sam Green said, "Call."

Albert Dark said, "I'm out," and laid his cards in front of him, face down.

Johnny tossed out two chips. "Raise you five."

Judge Tyler said, "Call the raise," and put in two chips.

Helgeson threw his cards away. Sam Green met the raise.

Judge Tyler asked Sam, "How many cards?"

Green said, "Three."

The judge dealt three cards, and Green picked them up, one at a time.

"Johnny?"

"Two," said Johnny.

Tyler said, "I'm taking one." He put one card from his hand on top of the cards remaining in the deck, and pushed them toward Helgeson. "Your bet, Sam."

Sam Green said, "I check."

"Johnny?"

"I'll tap you," Johnny said, and shoved in his remaining eighteen chips.

Tyler sighed and met the bet. Sam glowered at Johnny but also met the bet. They both looked at Johnny.

"Three queens," he said, and waited.

Tyler tossed his cards in and looked away. Sam Green slapped his cards angrily on the table but said nothing. Johnny looked at his own cards—a pair of nines and three odd cards—and tossed them in upside down. Helgeson picked them up without looking, and Johnny raked in the chips.

Helgeson began to shuffle. Johnny turned to Pearson, who was still behind him. "Something on your mind, mister?"

"Uh—no. No, I guess not."

Johnny turned back pleasantly. "Slow game tonight."

Helgeson dealt. The men looked at their cards, but there was no conversation at the table, no enthusiasm.

Sam Green said, "Open for—" he looked at Johnny— "ten?"

"Good bet," said Johnny.

Albert Dark looked at his hand, started to throw it away, then looked at Johnny and said, "I better call."

"I'll call," said Johnny.

Tyler threw in his cards. Helgeson called and asked, "How many cards?"

Sam took one, Albert three, Johnny three.

Sam said, "Bet twenty."

"I'll call," said Albert.

Johnny tossed his cards into the center. "It's too much for me," he grunted.

Helgeson turned his cards over.

Sam laid his cards down. Albert Dark looked at them and nodded. He tossed his cards in, and Sam picked up the chips. Then Sam gathered the cards, shuffled them, and dealt.

Albert Dark said, "Open for ten."

Johnny looked up. "Your ten and ten more."

"Call the twenty," said Tyler.

Helgeson mumbled, "Call."

Sam Green tossed in twenty dollars, and Albert Dark

called. Then Sam asked, "How many cards, gents?" and dealt them around. "The dealer takes two," he said finally, and looked at them. "Your bet, Albert."

"I check."

Johnny said, "Fifty."

Tyler frowned but said, "I call."

Helgeson, Sam Green, and Albert Dark called. They all looked at Johnny. He glanced at his hand, trying to decide what to do. Sometimes it wasn't much fun to play poker this way, but this was the way Red had shown him. He had a pair of fours and three odd cards. He hesitated, then looked up. "Three queens," he said.

They all tossed in their cards. Johnny threw his in face down and raked in the chips. Albert Dark picked up the cards and began to shuffle. Helgeson, broke, got up and left the table.

Johnny heard Pearson mutter something and toss down a drink. He got up from the table and went over to the bar. "Something bothering you, mister?"

Pearson looked at him, looked at his belt. "You carryin' a gun, mister?"

"No," said Johnny. "Never need one."

"Maybe you won't mind if I ask a question."

"Maybe."

"They play poker different in different parts of the country," Pearson began.

"Yes," said Johnny, "they play it different here too."

"And three queens—"

Johnny smiled. "When Red Concho's brother calls three queens, that's the end of that hand."

"Oh."

Johnny said sharply, "If you've got any more questions, mister, get 'em out of your system now."

"No. Not me." Pearson turned to the bar, and Johnny walked to his chair at the table. Albert Dark had finished dealing, and Johnny sat down and picked up his hand. He heard the swinging doors creak, and looked up.

Walker, one of the morning's two visitors to Cripple Creek, still in his blue shirt and levis, came in carrying a saddlebag. A little bowlegged, he stopped just inside the doors and looked all around the room. He saw Johnny, and Johnny raised his eyes to Walker's. He knew Walker recognized him, but the man gave no sign. With his two guns on his thighs, he finished looking over the room. Then he advanced a step.

The swinging doors creaked again, and Tallman came through, his outthrust jaw matching his hard eyes. He was still dressed in black, and he stood there for a moment, waiting. When nothing happened, he moved toward the bar. Walker dropped his saddlebag at the end of the bar, and joined him. Duke walked over and leaned sidewise against the bar. He said with a wry smile, "Howdy."

Benson and Pearson picked up their bottle and went to a table. Pearl was still sitting with the rancher.

Tallman said quietly, "You got a room?"

"And grub," said Walker. "We've done a lot of ridin' today. We're hungry."

"Whenever you're ready," said Duke.

Tallman said, "I'm thirsty."

Walker called out to Harry, "Set 'em up!"

Harry took a bottle off the shelf. He poured two shots and started to replace the bottle.

"Leave it!" Walker said.

Harry left it. Walker slid a glass toward Tallman, who reached for it without looking, tossed it down, and set the glass on the bar. "Is this the only action in town?" he asked Lang.

"There'll be more later," said Duke quickly. "Want to look at your room?"

Tallman asked, "How long before you fix something to eat?"

"Take about twenty minutes," said Duke.

"That's enough time for a few rounds of poker," said Tallman.

Duke sounded worried. "The town opens up when the hands come in off the range. Why don't you wait and pick a decent game?"

Walker poured two more drinks. He slid one toward Tallman, who again reached without looking and downed it.

"You want to sit in, Walker?" he asked.

"I'd rather see the room," said Walker. "The last one we had was alive."

"Good idea," said Duke quickly. "Come along, Mr.

Tallman. We got the finest rooms in this part of Arizona. We change sheets every week."

Tallman did not look at him. "Later," he said. He put his glass down and walked to the table. He stood and watched the game for a moment. Nobody looked up. He said, "You gents mind if I sit in?"

Albert Dark looked up at Tallman and then back at his cards.

"This is sort of a steady game," said Green.

"I see an open chair," said Tallman.

Judge Tyler spoke up. "Ordinarily we'd be glad to welcome you, but we're breaking up at the end of this round and it wouldn't be exactly fair."

Tallman was standing behind Johnny, and Johnny smiled quietly as they hunted excuses.

Tallman spoke in good humor. "I've seen the last round of many a game stretch into three days."

Sam Green said testily, "Later tonight you'll find some action—plenty of it."

Tallman said coldly, "That's the second time I've heard that. Now I'm waitin' to hear if there's any objection to my sittin' in."

He looked at Tyler, who dropped his eyes; at Sam Green, at Albert Dark. He started to speak to Johnny, who said without turning, "There's an empty chair."

"That's funny," said Tallman. "Nobody else at the table mentioned it."

Tallman walked around the table and sat down in Helgeson's chair opposite Johnny Concho. Tallman looked at Johnny and smiled. Johnny smiled back. Tallman looked at the chips in front of Johnny. "The cards seem to be running for you."

Johnny smiled and nodded.

Tallman, still looking at Johnny, said, "Walker!"

Walker stood behind Tallman's chair. Tallman, without moving his eyes from Johnny, held up his hand. Walker put a stack of gold coins in it. Tallman put the eagles and half-eagles in front of him.

Johnny said, "Your deal, Judge."

He was wondering just how much trouble he might have with these two men. Sixteen hours earlier he had ordered them out of town. Now they were back. Well, he'd give them a lesson. He picked up his cards and said idly, "Just riding through?"

"So far," said Tallman.

"Where you from?"

"You name it."

"Texas, by the sound of your voice."

"That's good enough," Tallman declared.

From where he was sitting, Johnny saw Duke lean over the bar and say something to Harry. Harry stripped off his apron and disappeared into the back. Then the door slammed, and Johnny smiled. Harry had gone to find the sheriff.

Duke walked casually to the table where Pearl sat with the rancher. "You better go upstairs," he said.

She looked up at him, and Johnny, watching her as the cards fell, did not understand her reaction. She said, "No, Duke, I'm staying." It wasn't her words that puzzled Johnny, but the look of strain on her face. His eyes dropped back to the cards as he considered it. One thing sure: it had made Pearl look suddenly older, and he realized that she was still a handsome woman. She must have had a hard life following Duke Lang around, he thought— and still she wasn't more than thirty-five.

Sam Green looked at his cards. "I'll open for ten," he said.

"Call," said Tallman.

Albert Dark said, "I'm out," but continued to study his cards.

"Throw them in," Tyler said sharply.

Dark dropped them suddenly as though they were hot, and looked up at Tyler in bewilderment.

Johnny said, "I raise it ten." He turned his eyes on the newcomer. "What do they call you?" he asked as if he hadn't heard.

"Tallman."

Tyler said, "I call."

Sam Green said, "I'm out."

Unexpectedly Tallman said, "Call the ten and raise you twenty."

Johnny smiled. "Your twenty and twenty more."

Tyler said slowly, "I call the two raises."

Tallman grinned as he dropped in two gold coins.

"Only one way to learn your game. I call."

"Cards?" said Tyler.

"One," said Tallman. He tossed out a card face down, picked up the new card and slipped it into his hand without looking.

"Johnny?" said Tyler.

Johnny held up two fingers.

"And the dealer takes two," said Tyler.

Tallman riffled the cards in his hand, glanced at them, and laid them on the table upside down. "I check."

Johnny looked at the pair of queens and three odd cards in his hand. He raised his eyes to Tallman's. "Fifty," he said.

Tyler shook his head. "I'm out."

Walker had gone around the table and was standing behind and a little to one side of Tallman. For an instant Johnny watched him, but he wasn't very much concerned.

Tallman looked at the pot and then at Johnny. "Let's make it worth while." Without looking, he held his open hand toward Walker, who dropped some coins in it. "Up a hundred," said Tallman.

Johnny said easily, "Your hundred and a hundred more."

The swinging doors gave off the small sound of rusty springs as Pete Henderson walked in. The sheriff came up to the table. Johnny glanced at him. The sheriff looked at Tyler, who shrugged. Then the sheriff walked over behind Johnny.

Tallman looked at his cards and then at Johnny. "A rough game you play, mister."

"You were looking for action," Johnny reminded him.

"Uh-huh," Tallman said absently, and studied Johnny. "You might be betting your hand—or you might be bluffing. Either way it's worth a hundred to find out." He pushed a pile of coins into the center.

Johnny smiled. "Three queens," he said.

Tyler sighed. Sam Green's lips were tight. Albert Dark kept his eyes on the table in front of him.

Tallman said, "That beats three nines." He spread his cards face up on the table. "They say it costs money to learn," he said casually.

Johnny smiled, "That's what they say." He folded his cards together and started to toss them into the center of the table, but Tallman leaned over abruptly and grabbed his wrist.

Johnny spoke with assurance. "I said three queens."

Tallman showed his teeth. "I learned the game in Kansas, and they taught me to show my cards."

Johnny said, "You're a long way from home, Tallman."

The man in black twisted Johnny's wrist, keeping it pinned on the table, and the cards fell face up. Tallman looked at them and said incredulously: "You mean *two* queens." He released Johnny's wrist and drew back in his chair.

"I said three queens," said Johnny. "In Cripple Creek that means I win."

Tallman moved suddenly. His right hand appeared on the table with a .44 Colt in it. Walker, behind him, was holding a six-shooter on the men at the bar, and he backed up slowly to cover also Pearl and the rancher at one table and Pearson and Benson at the other. Tallman pushed his chair back as he got up, not taking his eyes away from Johnny Concho.

Johnny laughed. "I guess you forget who I am."

Henderson said to Tallman: "He isn't wearin' guns."

Tallman backed a step. "I don't like to kill a man without iron—but I will."

Johnny looked at Tallman. The man wasn't taking the hint, and the muzzle end of his Colt looked pretty big. Johnny laughed nervously. "Somebody," he said to the crowd, "better tell this stranger who I am before he makes a mistake." He moistened his lips and looked at the men in the saloon. Pete Henderson opened his mouth as if to speak, but closed it again without saying anything. "Well?" demanded Johnny, and his eyes began to narrow as he met the circle of blank faces.

Walker said to the crowd, "Don't nobody else make a mistake. One a night is enough."

Tallman said to Johnny, "How do you want it, mister?"

Johnny answered, "I told you this morning my name is Johnny Concho."

Walker, not taking his eyes from the crowd, said out of the side of his mouth, "Mr. Tallman, make the acquaintance of the late Johnny Concho."

"I told you!" blurted Johnny. "My brother is Red Concho."

Tallman said ominously and without lowering his six-shooter, "Never heard of him."

"Never mind," Johnny said. "But it means that when I say I have three queens, I *have* three queens."

Tallman said in a gravelly voice, "That's poker?"

"In Cripple Creek," Johnny said, "we have our own rules."

"You hear that?" Tallman turned to Walker. "In Cripple Creek, if your brother is Red Concho, all you have to do is say three queens and you win the pot. House rule, he says."

"I heard," said Walker, looking at Johnny, "but somehow I ain't impressed."

"*Two* queens," Tallman said to Johnny in a harsh voice, and paused. "For Red Concho is dead!"

Johnny frowned. Then he realized what Tallman had said. He jumped up from the chair, staring at Tallman. "He's what?"

"Dead!" said Tallman.

"This afternoon," said Walker. "In a gun fight."

Johnny shouted: "You're lying! Nobody can outdraw my brother!"

Tallman said, his jaw outthrust: "One man proved he can."

"Who?" demanded Johnny.

Tallman said coldly: "The man who killed him."

"Who?" shouted Johnny.

"Me," said Tallman.

Johnny stared at him in disbelief. Then the full force of it hit him. He shuddered, and then anger at Tallman blazed through him. He started to leap across the table, but Pete Henderson thrust out a big arm and held him back.

Tallman grinned. "You almost died," he said, watching Johnny.

Henderson said, "You've got to give a man a chance."

Tallman spoke without moving his head: "Do I, Walker?"

"The sheriff says so," said Walker, and added, "but he ain't wearin' guns either."

"Then," said Tallman, "it don't look like I have to do nothing I don't want to do. If a man jumps across the table at me, I figure I might be justified in shooting him. How do you figure it, Walker?"

"Arizona law," said Walker.

"Of course," said Tallman, "this here's a special case. We was talkin' about men. Now I been watchin' this here youngun handle cards tonight, and I somehow got the idea he ain't no man, Walker. He's playin' at cards like a kid that ain't dry behind the ears. And I don't like to shoot a kid—but I would if I was pushed," he said, looking at Johnny.

Johnny stared at Pete Henderson. "You're the law. Say something!"

"You got it wrong, sonny." Tallman motioned with his Colt. "This says I'm the law in Cripple Creek."

Walker sneered. "I figured there'd be some fight in a brother of Red Concho."

Tallman said coldly to Johnny, "Your brother needed killin'. He needed it for a long time—and he got it, but I always like to do a little somethin' for the loser." He looked at the swinging doors. "So, you bein' his kid brother and all—you got till sunrise tomorrow. Either draw or run." He chucked his six-shooter in its holster and looked at Walker. "Put it away," he said. With contempt in his face, he walked past Johnny and went straight to Lang, keeping his back turned to Johnny. "You was right," he said. "There isn't much action in this town."

Walker had followed Tallman. "Let's see that room," he said.

Tallman hooked his thumbs in his belt. "We want the best you got."

Duke Lang moistened his lips and looked at Johnny. A flicker of triumph smouldered in his eyes, and he said to Tallman: "The best room is at the head of the stairs— overlooks the street."

"That's *my* room!" shouted Johnny.

Tallman didn't seem to hear him. "You sure it's the best?" he asked.

Duke Lang nodded without looking at Johnny.

"Then throw the kid's stuff out!" Tallman ordered.

Duke Lang nodded. He started up the stairway. Tallman and Walker went to the far end of the bar, picked up their saddlebags, and followed him.

There was a dead silence from those left in the room, and the harsh thumps of the two men's boot heels grated on Johnny's nerves. He waited until they were on the second floor. Then he turned to the men around him. "What are you going to do—just stand there?" He looked around, but no one answered.

Joe Helgeson had come from somewhere, and now he stared at Johnny as if he'd never seen him before. He was a head taller than Johnny, and when Johnny looked up at him appealingly, Helgeson snorted and walked away.

"Are you going to let them get away with it?" Johnny demanded, and still there was no answer. Johnny looked around wildly. "He killed my brother!" he said hoarsely.

Sam Green snorted and stamped out of the saloon.

Johnny turned to Tyler. "You're the judge. I let you be elected."

Tyler studied him for a moment. His face didn't change, but he went around the table and started for the door. Johnny shouted at him: "You heard him admit he murdered my brother!"

Tyler stopped and looked back, his eyes veiled. "He said he killed your brother. You're the one who used the word murdered," he pointed out.

Johnny turned in bewilderment to Pete Henderson. "You're the sheriff. It's your job!"

"My job is to keep the law," said Henderson.

"But he murdered—"

"Whatever he did, it didn't happen in my county," said Henderson.

Benson and Pearson, seeming considerably puzzled by all that had happened, went out, and Albert Dark, his eyes on the floor to avoid Johnny's, followed them.

Johnny looked around the room. Harry, the bartender, was rinsing glasses. Pete Henderson still stood by the table. The rancher at the table with Pearl had gone out, and suddenly the big room seemed very empty and Johnny felt very much alone. He looked up at Henderson, pleading. "You can't let a murderer walk the streets," he said.

Johnny looked at Pearl, and noticed for the first time

that she didn't seem to be against him as were all the others, for on her face, now strangely soft, was a look of concern.

Henderson idly picked up Johnny's hand. "You called your cards wrong," he said.

Johnny snatched the cards out of his hand and threw them on the floor. "What difference does that make?"

The sheriff looked toward the room upstairs. "It made a difference to him." He looked at Johnny. "Your three queens call made a difference to *us* too, but we didn't do anything about it. Nobody had the courage to say he didn't like it."

"Red—"

Henderson interrupted him. "The way it adds up to me, Cripple Creek made the mistake a lot of towns make: the people didn't get together and act like a town."

"My brother—"

"Nobody," Henderson said emphatically, "can buffalo a whole town when the people act together." He looked upstairs again. "That's something we may still have to learn."

"You're the sheriff," said Johnny. "You—"

"No sheriff can do it by himself. A sheriff is only as big as the will of the people—and in Cripple Creek I reckon that isn't very big."

"That isn't fair, Pete," Pearl said in a soft voice.

Henderson looked at her. "Yes, ma'am, I reckon it's fair. Cripple Creek will never take its rightful place as a town until somebody shows the way—somebody who isn't afraid to risk his neck, if necessary." The sheriff turned and walked heavily out of the saloon.

Johnny called to Harry: "Pour me a drink, Harry!"

Harry raised up from dish-washing and looked at Johnny. Very deliberately he dried his hands on his apron; then he turned and went back into the kitchen.

Chapter Four

JOHNNY SAT THERE, trying to understand. Pearl came over and stood by the table. "What's happened, Pearl?" he asked. "The people—" He shook his head in bewilderment. "What's happened to the people in this town?"

Pearl touched his arm. Her voice was low. "They're confused, Johnny. They don't know what to think. They don't understand, Johnny."

"Don't understand what?"

"That you are really just a little boy."

"I'm of age," he said, looking at her.

She nodded. "Yes, Johnny, but you've always been Red Concho's little brother—and that has made a difference."

He heard hard boot heels on the floor above, and Tallman came down the stairs with his arms full of Johnny's clothes. He dropped them on the floor by Johnny's table and went back upstairs.

Johnny looked at the clothes and then up the stairs. "The town won't take this lying down," he said suddenly, "and neither will I."

"What can you do?" asked Pearl.

"There's plenty of guns in Cripple Creek. I'll find enough to back me up."

Pearl looked toward the stairway. "He gave you time. You'd better not waste a minute of it."

Johnny got up. "We'll see who's boss of Cripple Creek," he said, and went outside.

It was dark, but the stars were brilliant in a vast, blue-black sky. A few yellow lights burned along the street, and two saddle horses were tied in front of Albert Dark's store, but there was no one on the street. He looked both ways indecisively. Then he walked rapidly toward the glowing red forge he could see in Helgeson's blacksmith shop.

Helgeson was leaning against the anvil, his arms folded.

"I've got to talk to you!" said Johnny.

"Air is cheap," said Helgeson. "Talk."

At that moment Johnny realized he didn't feel very

sure of himself, but he went on, "You know what I want."

"You always wanted something, Johnny. What is it this time?"

"Are you going to let a strange gunfighter push you around?" Johnny demanded.

"He gave *you* eight hours," Helgeson pointed out. "Not *me.*"

"You can handle a gun," said Johnny. "I've seen you."

"I take care of myself," said Helgeson.

Johnny sensed the immovability of the man, and turned aimlessly. In the flickering firelight he saw only one saddle on the wall—the gold-ornamented saddle. He turned back to Helgeson. "What happened to the silver saddle—*my* saddle?"

"I put it away," said Helgeson.

"I always kept it right here, across the door from the gold saddle."

Helgeson nodded, his eyes half-closed. "You never paid for it," he said implacably.

"You mean you're taking back—" He heard the whinny of a horse from the stable. "That's the black!" he said, and ran to the gate. Somebody, mounted on the black, was riding through the other gate. Johnny ran through the stable and into the alley. The rider was bringing the horse around to face him, and Johnny ran up and grabbed the reins. "Sam Green!" he exclaimed. "Sam, I need this horse!"

"What horse?" Sam asked coldly.

Johnny's voice was high. "This horse—it's mine!"

"You got a bill of sale?" asked Sam. "A receipt for the money?" He paused and then said bitterly, "You never paid for anything, Johnny. You don't own anything." He leaned far over and yanked the reins from Johnny's hand. Then he spurred the horse into a gallop, and Johnny stood there until the plopping sound of the hoofbeats in the dusty road had died away. Then he went slowly back through the stable and into the blacksmith shop.

Helgeson was still there, his great bare torso red in the light from the forge. "It doesn't look like you've got much use for a saddle now," he said.

Johnny clenched his fists and moved toward him. Helgeson made no motion, but his eyes looked hard.

Johnny turned back. He ran down the street to the general store and stopped before the door, puffing. He put his hand to the doorknob but stopped as Sarah Dark, inside, pulled down the shade that said "Closed." He worked at the door but it was locked. He ran heavily along the path to another board sidewalk, and burst in at a door that bore the legend: "Earl Tyler. Attorney."

The judge was leaning against the edge of his desk. "Want something, Johnny?"

"I need help, Judge."

Tyler's face showed no sympathy. "A little legal advice? I'm rusty on wills and last testaments, but if you'll give me a few days to brush up—"

He reached toward Johnny's vest and slipped the gold watch out of its pocket. He unbuttoned the button and pulled the chain through, then held it in front of him and let the watch spin as the chain unwound.

Johnny's words were intense. "The whole town has got to stick together, Judge. Red had a lot of friends here and I'm counting on them to back me up."

Tyler dropped the watch in his vest pocket and threaded the chain through the button hole. "My father carried this watch for thirty years, and gave it to me when I came West," he said. "I've missed it."

Johnny said, "Who made you justice of the peace in Cripple Creek?"

Tyler took the watch from his vest pocket and rubbed his fingers over the soft gold case. "You see this scratch? That was from an Apache arrow. Got it down near Fort Bowie. Fellow next to me in the stagecoach was a lawyer. Refused to pay any attention to the Indians; kept readin' Blackstone. One arrow glanced off this watch and went halfway through his body—head stickin' out on one side, feathers on the other. He groaned and laid across my lap, his book still in his hand. The next arrow that came along was stopped by the book instead of my heart. So I decided to be a lawyer."

"Earl Tyler!" shouted Johnny. "Listen to me!"

Tyler sat down at his desk and picked up a book. He looked up at Johnny. "The section on wills is a little complicated. Give me a couple of days."

Johnny turned and walked out slowly. His shoulders

felt unspeakably heavy, for in all of Cripple Creek he was
alone. He walked back, head down. There was a light in
the window of his old room, but he didn't look up, for he
knew that Tallman was watching him. He found his way
to the sheriff's office and went inside.

Pete Henderson, his hat pushed back, said: "I've been
expecting you, Johnny."

Johnny said in bewilderment, "They want to see me
killed."

"I know."

"They took my saddle—my horse—everything. They
stripped me clean."

"Made up your mind about what you're going to do,
Johnny?"

Johnny looked up. "I guess you don't understand. They
cleaned me out."

"You're lookin' for somebody to do the job you were
supposed to do," said Henderson. "They took only what
belonged to them."

"There must be somebody in this town—"

"To fight your battles?" Henderson shook his head.

Johnny went on, not understanding. "Everybody used
to talk about Red—what a great guy he was. Now he's
dead and it's like they didn't even know him."

"It isn't often," Henderson suggested, "you get a chance
to meet the man who killed your own brother."

"What am I supposed to do about it?"

Pete Henderson looked at him, slowly shaking his head.

"He's a professional," Johnny said jerkily. "Killing is his
business. I wouldn't have a chance."

"I reckon not." The sheriff looked at the window.
"It's gettin' late."

"Is that all you've got to say?" Johnny demanded.

Pete Henderson settled back. "To tell you the truth,
Johnny, you got so little time, I don't figure you ought
to waste it talkin'."

Johnny said indignantly, "I can't draw with a gunslinger. I'd get killed."

Henderson nodded. "Likely."

Through the window Johnny saw lights in front of the
Copper Diggin's; he heard men talking and saw the stage
had pulled up in front of the saloon.

Johnny said, watching the stage, "Maybe I *won't* waste time talkin'."

"You'll have to ride a long way to forget what happened here."

"When I'm ready," Johnny said, "I'll be back."

"I'm not sure I can wait that long," said Pete Henderson.

Johnny left the sheriff's office, and went across the street. Milo tossed a limp mailbag up to the guard.

Pearson and Benson, conspicuous in their Eastern clothes, came out of the hotel. Pearson said, "I thought you didn't drive at night."

"We don't generally," said Milo, and threw a full carpetbag to the guard.

"Then why tonight?"

Milo was up-ending a suitcase. "Mister," he said, "this town ain't healthy."

The guard called down, "Come on with that suitcase."

Milo lifted it to the top of the stagecoach, and the guard took it out of his hands.

"It should be something to see," said Pearson, "when the town decides to stick up for its rights."

"You write me about it, mister!"

Johnny said to Milo, "You've got another passenger."

"We pull out in ten minutes," Milo warned.

The guard called down, "And we don't wait, Mr. Concho."

"I'll be here," Johnny said, but added as he turned to Pearson, "unless you gentlemen object to me riding with you."

Pearson shrugged. "It's a public carrier," he said.

Johnny went toward the door of the saloon. Tallman and Walker were leaning against the wall, one on each side of the door. Johnny stopped momentarily, then went forward. But as he reached the door, Tallman stretched his arm across, barring the way.

"You leaving, sonny?"

Johnny kept his eyes on the open door.

Walker said, "The man was talkin' to you."

Johnny didn't turn.

Tallman said, "You think he's scared deaf, Walker?"

"It looks that way."

"That won't bother him," said Tallman. "All he can hear is three queens."

"Sonny said he was leavin' town," said Walker.

"Pardon *me!*" said Tallman, and drew his arm back. "But remember, Johnny Concho, it's open season after sunrise tomorrow."

They both laughed, and Johnny went through the door, his face burning. He heard Tallman say harshly, "All right, Walker. He's leavin'. Round up the town. We'll have a meetin' as soon as the stage pulls out."

Duke Lang was behind the bar. Mrs. Brown's husband, with big hands gnarled from a lifetime of driving, was playing cards with two ore wagon drivers from the mountains. Pearl was sitting on the bottom step of the stairs, and she looked up as Johnny went by. "I put your things in the room next to Mr. Tallman, Johnny." There was a pause. "There isn't much time. I'll help you pack."

She followed him up. She lit the lamp, put the chimney on, and adjusted the wick. He was staring at the pile of clothes on the bed.

"Listen, Johnny!"

Pearl's voice was unexpectedly fierce, and he turned to look at her. "What is it?"

"Johnny, you never knew this, but I was in love with your brother once."

"Red?" he asked incredulously.

"Yes, Red Concho. He never told you, did he?"

"He never talked much about his own business."

"It's true," she said.

He studied her. "I guess I see how Red could be in love with you," he said slowly.

"We—had a fight and lost track of each other for a while. That's when I took up with Duke." She held Johnny by both arms. "I want you to take me with you, Johnny. I've got to get away from Duke."

"Duke!"

"He won't care. All he ever cared was that I would sit and talk to the customers and get them to buy more drinks. Johnny, you've got to take me with you."

He was amazed to see tears in her eyes. "Well, look. I—well, you can go on the stagecoach. It's a public carrier. But I—well, I haven't got enough money to take both of us to the next town."

"I've got money," she said, and pulled a buckskin bag from her bosom. "Gold! All my own! There's enough to take us anywhere—San Francisco, Alaska—"

"Well, now, look, Pearl. I—there's Mary Dark. I—"

She shook him fiercely. "A baby!" she said. "A green kid! You need somebody to mother you—somebody who knows the ropes. I can help you, Johnny. Please let me help you."

It was a little too fast for him. "Pearl, I—Duke—"

"I'll take care of it," she said quickly. "Here, put your things into this carpetbag. I'll go get my own things ready." She kissed him on the lips and went out without a sound.

He was confused, but if Pearl was going to leave on the same stage with him, he ought by all means to see Mary and tell her how things were. He began to put his clothes into the carpetbag, and then, hearing Milo ask, "What time you got, Judge?" he piled everything in and was just tucking in the loose ends when he heard the door close behind him. "Pearl—" he said.

"It ain't Pearl," said Joe Helgeson's heavy voice.

Johnny turned. "Joe! What do you want?"

"The talk is you're leaving, Johnny."

Johnny backed a step. "Who told you?"

"On the stage. Is that true?"

Johnny turned to close the carpetbag.

Helgeson's voice said behind him, "You better get used to answerin' questions, Johnny."

Johnny whirled around. "I'm gettin' out, Helgeson. That straight enough for you?"

"It's an answer," Helgeson said dryly.

Johnny turned back and looked around the room. There wasn't much to see, for all his things had been in the pile on the bed. He closed the carpetbag and started for the door.

But Helgeson was still there. He jerked the carpetbag out of Johnny's hand and threw it onto the bed. Johnny backed a step and watched Helgeson as the big man returned to the door and put his back against it.

"Get out of my way!" said Johnny.

Helgeson said harshly, "You're not leavin', Johnny—not right now. You're not goin' to cheat me out of this."

Johnny frowned and started for him. The big man laid heavy hands on his arms, spun him around, and shoved him toward the bed. Johnny stumbled, caught himself, and fell over the bed but immediately got up. He turned around, and Helgeson hit him in the face and slammed him back on the bed. Johnny got one elbow under him, shook his head, wiped the blood from his chin, and started to get up. Helgeson waited. Johnny got to his feet and took a swing at Helgeson, who hit him in the mouth with a big fist that felt like a piledriver. Johnny landed back on the bed. He heard the driver's "Heyeee-iiii!" The sound shook the cobwebs out of his head and he rolled over on his stomach and crawled across the bed to the open window. "Wait!" he called. "Wait for me!"

But he heard the crack of the whip, the creak of leather, and the rubbing of wood, and then the crunching sound of iron tires in the sandy dirt. Johnny got up from the bed and stood reeling. "Get out of my way!" he said.

He stumbled toward Helgeson, fighting to keep his balance. Helgeson said, "No, Johnny."

But Johnny reached the door. Helgeson caught his shoulder in one big hand, spun him around, and slammed him against the wall. Johnny kept his balance and started toward Helgeson, who pulled open the door to hit him full in the face. Johnny backed against the wall, partially dazed. Helgeson closed the door and Johnny pushed himself away from the wall. Helgeson pulled the door against him hard. It hit him on the forehead, and Johnny reeled backward and slumped to the floor. Helgeson walked over and picked him up. He led Johnny to the bed and set him down. Johnny slid backward. Helgeson looked at him for a moment and then turned and walked to the other side of the room. He took a chair, turned it around, and straddled it. Johnny, shaking his head, was breathing heavily.

Somebody knocked on the door, and Helgeson said, "Come."

The door opened and Pete Henderson came in. He was wearing a gun for the first time Johnny could remember. Helgeson asked, "Is everybody downstairs?"

"Almost," said Henderson, and nodded to Johnny. "What happened to him?"

"He fell off Flagstaff Mountain." He got up from his chair. "If you need any help I'll be downstairs."

Henderson looked at Johnny. "I won't need any help."

Chapter Five

HELGESON clumped out of the room. Henderson walked to the wash basin and let the water run until it was two-thirds full. He went over to Johnny and pulled him to his feet, guided him to the wash basin, and forced his head down. He held it there until Johnny began to struggle. Johnny raised his head and gasped for breath, and the sheriff tossed him a towel. Johnny wiped his face.

"You tried to kill me!" he gasped.

Henderson sat on the window sill. "I'm about the only one in town who isn't interested in doing just that, the way I see it."

"They won't even let me leave," said Johnny.

"Did you think they would?"

"I didn't think they'd help a stranger against one of their own."

"You've never been one of us, Johnny."

Johnny frowned. "Me and Red—all the badmen in Arizona were afraid of us. We—"

Henderson was shaking his head. "You got it wrong, Johnny. Nobody was ever afraid of *you*."

"You got nerve, sayin' that!"

"It's right, Johnny. Red had a gun—a gun that killed. Every gunslinger in the territory was afraid of it, so we waved it over Cripple Creek to keep them away."

"You hid behind it!"

Henderson nodded. "It took some doin'. Your brother liked to move around—so we had to keep an anchor on him. We kept you, Johnny."

Johnny laughed derisively. "You didn't keep me here. I coulda left any time I felt like it."

"We made sure you didn't," said Henderson. "The stuff you charged at Albert Dark's store—the horse you got from Sam—the drinks downstairs—the money you won playin' three queens—we each paid our share. You were a tax assessment like for a school or a sewer." He reached into his vest pocket and took out a slip and gave it to Johnny. "We all got receipts," he said. "Tax for Johnny

49

Concho—one a month. I got a drawer full of them if you want to see what you cost me personally."

Johnny crumpled the paper in his hand. "Why didn't somebody tell me I was livin' on charity?" he asked, his voice taut.

"At first," said Henderson, "we thought it was worth it." He looked at the wadded-up receipt that Johnny had dropped on the floor. "But the way it turned out, you made 'em swallow a lot for that piece of paper."

Johnny said belligerently, "Some day I'll make you all eat dirt."

"You'll have to work on Tallman first." He paused. "Johnny, I feel I still owe your brother something, since I used his gun to back up my star." He pushed his hat farther back on his head. "I'm going to help you, son."

Johnny said skeptically, "I sure believe that."

Henderson said, "You never thought much of me as a sheriff, did you, Johnny?"

"I never thought much of you as anything."

The sheriff looked at him without animosity. "Nobody does, I guess. But I wore a star through Abilene and Dodge City when them Texas cattle came up the trail. There ain't many men past fifty can say that." He paused. "I met a lot of gunslingers, kid. All of them faster than me—and I buried them all."

"I didn't ask for your life story," said Johnny.

Henderson went on: "The gunmen they tell stories about always had something special to give them an edge. Bill Hardin had a hideout gun; Jesse kept his holster tilted; Ringo wore 'em loose. And I outlived them all."

Johnny was watching him, impressed by the sincerity in Henderson's voice. Now the sheriff laid one hand on the butt of his six-shooter. He made a motion—not a draw, but a movement straight forward, and Johnny was looking into the muzzle of the pistol. "Look here," Henderson said. "See how the holster is split? There's a spring keeps the two halves together, and the gun hangs inside by a metal clip, like some of the old shoulder-holster pistols." He turned loose of the holster and the halves snapped back into place. He opened them again and showed Johnny how the gun hung in place, and once more demonstrated how it flipped straight out, saving a vital fraction of a second. "I wasn't faster," said Henderson. "I was just smarter."

He unbuckled the gunbelt and tossed it to Johnny, who caught it and buckled it on. He settled it solidly on his hips.

"Now!" said Henderson. "Use it!"

Johnny snatched at the gun butt. It came out of the holster smoothly and without a catch, and in the same motion it was buried in the sheriff's middle. Wide-eyed, Johnny looked at the gun. "It works!" He tried it again, and it went still more smoothly. "Fast!" he said wonderingly. "It works fast."

"It's never lost," said Henderson. "All you need is the guts to reach for it." He said quietly, "I'm bettin' you won't make it, kid."

Henderson left, and Johnny looked down at the holster. It had never lost, Henderson said. Johnny reached for it to practice, but in the very motion he remembered Tallman's hard face and eyes, and he froze. He tried to force himself to finish the draw, but he couldn't. He walked over to the window and back, and then, not daring to try it again, went out the door to the head of the stairs.

He saw Mary Dark standing on the bottom step, and the saloon was filled with the people of Cripple Creek: Josh, the swamper; Duke Lang, Mrs. Brown, Sam Green and two of his cowhands, Judge Tyler, Albert and Sarah Dark, Joe Helgeson, and twenty more. Johnny heard Tallman's voice: "This all of 'em?" and Walker's answer: "Not much of a town."

Johnny moved to where he could see the black-shirted Tallman standing on top of the bar, with Walker below him.

"Anybody object to this meeting?" asked Tallman.

Nobody spoke. Then Walker, below him, shook his head. "They're peaceful, cooperating folks."

Tallman's gravelly voice rang out. "You got a nice town, folks. Me and Walker are going to live here. When we live in a town we like to be happy, and the only way we can be happy is if nobody crosses us." He looked around at them all, then at Walker. "Think they understand?"

Walker said: "Better make it real plain, so there won't be any complaints."

Tallman said, "I gunned Red Concho, and that means what was his, is mine—namely, this town." He looked toward the stairs, but Johnny was still out of sight in the dark. "Unless his brother objects." He looked back at the crowd. "And I don't think he will. What about the rest of you folks?"

There was no answer.

Tallman jumped down easily from the bar and walked up to Henderson. "Sheriff, you got anything to say?"

Henderson looked at him but he didn't answer.

"Smart man," said Tallman. "Some people talk too much. Give me your badge."

There was a gasp from the crowd, and Henderson for a moment seemed unable to move.

"Give it to me," Tallman said coldly.

The sheriff took it off slowly and handed it to Tallman. The man looked at it, then pinned it on his black shirt. "Bein' the top-hand around here, folks, I appoint myself sheriff and I solemnly swear to do my duty." He looked around. "In the meantime I want twenty cents out of every dollar that comes into this town. Is that clear?" He waited to let it sink in. "Silver, cattle, stores, everything. You got a bank?"

Nobody answered.

"Then start one," he said, "because I'm the new president. Any objections?"

From where Johnny stood he could see Sam Green's face working. Sam was fighting mad. Albert Dark looked scared that there would be violence. Judge Tyler seemed resigned. Henderson stood stiffly, staring at the wall. Joe Helgeson's big chest swelled up as he took in this development. Duke Lang looked pale in the lamplight. Pearl was nowhere in sight.

Tallman pointed a finger at Duke. "You!"

"Yes?"

"Me and my partner are guests here from now on."

Duke smiled thinly. "By a strange coincidence," he said, "you're living in the guest room."

Tallman moved back to the bar. "I'm fair. I don't take unless I can give something back."

He whirled, his movements catlike, and whipped out a six-shooter. "This will see that no gunslinger shoots up the town." He whipped out his second pistol. "Any of you start fightin' among yourselves—this will settle it, fair and square." He grinned and pointed with his pistol to the two on Walker's hips. "Those will see that nobody tries to settle *me*."

Johnny had started quietly down the stairs. He hit a step that creaked, and Walker, looking up, exclaimed: "Well, look who's here!"

Every head in the room turned to Johnny. Tallman said slowly, "The last of the Conchos—and carryin' a gun too." He said it wonderingly, the same as he had called Johnny's queens—not quite sure of what he would find out, Johnny knew, but at the same time not afraid. Johnny swallowed as Tallman walked up to face him at the foot of the stairs. Mary stepped down and turned to watch Johnny. Henderson turned, nothing showing on his face. Helgeson looked up hopefully. Judge Tyler saw the gun but did not seem to take hope. Albert Dark looked scared.

Tallman said, "You want somethin', little man?"

Johnny tried to answer but could not force the words out of his mouth.

Tallman's voice was harsh. "Because if you don't—I told you to git out of town."

Johnny tried to speak but couldn't. He tried to force his hand toward the gun, to drive it there, but his muscles were paralyzed.

Tallman stood in his way like an iron colossus. "Now you gonna lay on that steel or are you gonna crawl?"

"Use it, Johnny!" Henderson whispered. "Use it!"

Johnny tried again but his hand would not move. He saw Mary stifle a scream, and in his own mind he seemed to be screaming too, though he knew he wasn't making a sound. He took one more step and stopped.

"What do you say, sonny?" Tallman's eyes were narrow and watchful, but Johnny could have told him, if he could have talked, that Tallman had nothing to be scared of; that he, Johnny Concho, couldn't draw a gun to kill no matter how much he wanted to. He took one more step, and said hoarsely, "I need a horse."

"So you can run?" asked Tallman.

Johnny looked at him but didn't answer.

"Say it, sonny. Say it!"

The driving force of the man, more than the threat of his guns, beat Johnny down. "So I can run," he said finally.

Tallman smiled a hard smile and looked around the room. He grinned and turned back to Johnny. "Okay, sonny, take my horse. I'll pick up a better one."

Johnny took one last look around the room. The faces of the people were cold, impassive, ashamed. He took the last step down and started for the door. Then Tallman's gravelly voice said, "Turn around, sonny."

Johnny hesitated, then slowly turned.

Tallman's eyes were on him. "Deputy Walker, ain't there a law about kids carryin' guns?"

"There sure is, Sheriff."

Tallman drew and fired in the same motion. For an instant Johnny thought the sound of the explosion and the smell of powdersmoke would free him from his fear, but then he felt the jerk at his waist, and knew the sheriff's gun had been shot away.

Tallman grinned through the powdersmoke and replaced his pistol. "Good-by, sonny."

Johnny paused, looked around at the hostile faces, then turned and plunged through the door. He heard Mary cry, "Johnny! Johnny!" but he could not stop. He saw Tallman's horse standing outside, its reins on the ground. He ran to it. He couldn't face Mary now. He threw the reins over the horse's head and swung into the saddle as the horse turned in a tight circle. He saw Mary framed for an instant in the yellow light of the doorway, heard her call.

"Johnny, don't run! Don't run, Johnny!"

Thoroughly ashamed, and bitter with himself and his helpless muscles, he jammed his heels into the horse's flanks and rode out of town at full speed. He looked back once, to see Mary standing in the street in front of the Copper Diggin's. Then he laid down along the horse's neck and raked its flanks with his heels. He could never in all his life, he felt, live down the shame and humiliation of that moment when he had had a gun—he, the brother of Red Concho—and had not been able to use it.

Chapter Six

AFTER A WHILE he let the horse slow down to a walk, and rode along in the dark, trying to figure it out. Red had never been afraid of anybody—not even when he was thirteen years old. Why had he, Red's brother, been unable to draw a pistol?

Maybe it was because he'd never tried before; he'd never faced a gunslinger. Maybe he needed practice. Maybe it was because he'd been protected by Red all his life, and he hadn't ever thought about using a six-shooter on somebody else. Well, he realized grimly, it was time to start thinking. Red wasn't there any more, and Red couldn't watch out for him. For a little while he felt uneasy, thinking about Red and how Red had always taken care of him. He hadn't seen much of Red in the last few years, but Red had always been behind him.

Red had been behind him all his life, even in school. He remembered when Red had bought him a new pair of pants with buckles that fastened just below the knees, and the biggest boy in Johnny's grade had made fun of him because he said the pants were too tight. Maybe the pants *were* a little tight, but Johnny had been so excited over them that he hadn't paid any attention to the fit. His old pants were ragged and worn, and Johnny had patched them with blue denim—the only thing they had—and had worn them to school, aware of them but unable to do anything about it. Then one day Red counted out two dollars in nickels and dimes and said, "Go buy yourself some new ones, Johnny." He said almost fiercely, "You're a Concho. You got to look nice." Johnny went down and bought the new ones, skin-tight, maybe, but undeniably new. And then the big boy began to make fun of him.

Red went down and raised cain with the storekeeper, but the man said Johnny had insisted on that pair, and now he had worn them and there was nothing he could do.

The big boy continued to taunt Johnny, and one day at noon when they were lined up to go inside, the boy began to chant, "Johnny Skin-tight! Johnny Skin-tight!"

When Johnny, almost in tears, told Red about it, Red said grimly, "We'll take care of him." The next afternoon, on the way home, Red caught the boy and rassled with him and threw him into a clump of prickly pear, and they told it around town that the doctor spent half the night pulling stickers out of the boy's legs, and he limped for a long time.

Johnny felt sorry for him, but Red said fiercely, "Nobody can make fun of a Concho."

It wasn't long after that that Red got a gunbelt and a gun and began to practice drawing. The town marshal tried to take the gun away from him, but Red got away and hid out in the desert. He came back for Johnny at night, and they packed up their few belongings and left town, riding double on an old sway-backed gray horse that Red had got from the livery.

There was a long succession of towns. Some stays were short, some long. People tried to take Johnny away from Red, but when they got too insistent, Red and Johnny moved on.

Red became real good with his gun, and when a committee of citizens, headed by a deputy sheriff, came to take Johnny away with them and put him in somebody's home, Red outdrew the deputy and held them all off while Johnny threw their things into a saddlebag and they got out of town.

After that, Johnny wanted to buy himself a gun and learn to use it, but Red said no emphatically. "You wouldn't hurt a fly," he said to Johnny, "and I don't want you to start. You're no killer, Johnny. You'd only get killed." Red, with his sandy hair and his freckled face, shook his head and said earnestly, "I'll do the gunslingin' in the Concho family, Johnny. You be the one who is respectable and law-abidin'. Some day you'll be a businessman, and marry and raise a family. That's your job, Johnny. My job is to see you get the chance. And no damn snooty people are goin' to take over and make a stableboy or a swamper out of you."

"Maybe," said Johnny, "these people are trying to look out for us."

"They ain't," said Red positively. "They want to put you to work washin' dishes and cuttin' wood and carryin' out ashes. We don't need no help," Red said stubbornly. "I'm lookin' out for both of us."

Eventually they came to Cripple Creek, a town that had started up because they thought the railroad would run a spur through it from the copper mines. But the railroad went instead to Silver City, and Cripple Creek settled down to a quiet existence until Doc Murchison came along. He'd been run out of Socorro for killing a miner, and he swaggered up and down the one street of Cripple Creek, roaring drunk, shooting windows and scaring people half to death, and finally shooting Pete Henderson in the arm when Pete tried to make him behave.

Everybody but Red was scared of Doc, and one day when Doc was shooting up the Copper Diggin's, Red buckled on his gun and went to stop him.

They met in the Copper Diggin's, with Doc Murchison at the bar and Red standing just inside the swinging doors.

"I thought I told everybody in Cripple Creek to leave off the hardware," Doc said, sizing up Red and his sandy hair.

Red was small and slim, but his blue eyes bored into Doc Murchison's and he said, "That means you too, Doc."

Doc snorted and said, "A boy! A damn' milk-suckin' boy, tellin' *me* what to do."

"Take off your gunbelt," Red said, and his high-pitched voice penetrated every part of the Copper Diggin's, and nobody made a move.

Doc turned back to the bar. Red stood there, waiting, his hands at his sides. Doc took a drink. Then he threw the glass into the mirror and drew his gun in the same movement.

But he was too late. Red had drawn and fired, and the bullet caught Doc in the breastbone, and his gun-arm slowly dropped as he looked at Red, who was waiting with his gun pointed and a cloud of smoke rising from it.

Doc fell back against the bar and gradually slipped to the floor.

He died that night, and Red packed to leave. "It's only a question of time," he said to Johnny, "until the sheriff will come after me from Silver City."

Johnny said, bewildered, "It was a fair fight."

"Sure," said Red, "but a jury might not see it that

way. You never know. I been watchin' these things while you was growin' up. I know how it goes. It will be better for me to move on. I don't like jails, Johnny. I never will." He fastened the buckle on his saddlebag. "I want you to stay right here. I won't be far—never too far. I want you to take care of Cripple Creek. Me killing Doc Murchison, and you stayin' here with everybody knowin' you're my brother, will mean that no gunslinger will dare to come in here and take over the way Doc tried to do."

"What'll I do to get money to live on?"

"You seen me play three queens?" asked Red.

"Sure."

"Whenever you need some money, these people will play with you. You can buy whatever you want and charge it. I'll settle up some day."

"What if they don't want to do that?"

"It ain't what they want," said Red. "It's what they've got to do—and they know it. Nobody here can take care of this town. Pete Henderson is too old. They'll be glad to take care of you so they'll know where I stand. And the word will go out that Red Concho is watchin' over Cripple Creek, and if there's any trouble I'll be back. Meantime don't worry about me, Johnny. I'll write you once a month."

So Red had gone on, and within a few months he blazed a trail through western Arizona. He became known as the top gunhand in Arizona Territory. Occasionally somebody came along to dispute the title, and they buried him in the cactus. They said that sometimes Red used a bullwhip instead of a gun, but Johnny didn't know about that.

Now that he thought about it, he didn't know much about Red at all in his last few years, except that all over Arizona Territory, Red Concho's name threw fear into people.

Red moved a lot until he more or less settled at Holbrook, but even then he never stayed right in town very long. His last letter or two—he nearly always wrote on the first of the month, and they weren't long letters, but he asked how Johnny was getting along and if he needed anything—his last letter or two had come from Rawhide, a town about a day's ride from Holbrook.

Johnny stopped after a while to give the horse a breather. A chill had come down from the mountains, and the desert was cold. He walked the horse to keep it from stiffening up. Presently he stopped to build a fire out of some pine driftwood that had washed down from the mountains. He had nothing to eat, but the heat felt good on his face and hands, and he sat there for a while, occasionally hearing a coyote bark or an owl hoot somewhere out in the brush, but thinking nothing of it.

He could not understand why they all had refused help when he needed it against Tallman. He, Johnny Concho, had protected the town of Cripple Creek for a long time. They might have helped him just once. And the fury of Joe Helgeson—Johnny shuddered. His mouth was sore where Joe had hit him.

He was still wearing Pete Henderson's gunbelt, but it wasn't much good without a six-shooter and holster. He took it off, looked at the .38 cartridges in it, fingered one of them, and finally draped the belt over a clump of sagebrush. Standing there away from the fire, he heard the steady clop of a trotting horse, and looked quickly at his fire. It was too late to try to put it out. His horse, too, was out of reach, and Johnny faded back a little into the brush.

The sound came closer. The horse blew dust out of its nostrils, and Johnny's horse whinnied. The approaching horse slowed down to a walk, and a woman's voice called: "Johnny! Johnny Concho!"

Johnny stared into the dark. It sounded like Pearl. The horse came into the light of the fire, and it *was* Pearl. Johnny went forward to meet her.

"Oh, Johnny!" she said. "I'm so very glad you're all right."

"I'm all right," he said, and helped her dismount. Her body was warm where it touched his arms.

"I brought blankets," she said. "I knew you wouldn't have any."

"You might as well get warm," he said. "But what are you doing here?"

"I told you I wanted to go with you, Johnny. I told you how it was between Red and me."

"Sure, but—I'm not Red."

"I just want to look out for you, Johnny. You need somebody to look after you. Red always did that, didn't he?"

"Sure. Red always told me what to do, but—" He shook his head. "You're welcome to travel with me, Pearl, but Duke isn't gonna like it."

She put her head on his shoulder. "Duke won't care, Johnny. Duke hasn't cared about me for years."

He nodded. "All right. Suit yourself." He thought of Mary. "I don't reckon I'll ever see Cripple Creek again, and if I did I don't think anybody in the whole town would care."

"That's sensible, Johnny. They never thought much of you in Cripple Creek, but I've been watchin' you for a long time."

He got up. "We'd better unpack those blankets. It'll be cold toward morning."

"Whatever you say, Johnny."

He laid her carpetbag on top of a clump of sagebrush and brought the blankets back toward the fire. "One thing more, Pearl. You're married to Duke, and so you and I are strictly on a business basis."

She yawned. "All right, Johnny. You're safe with me anyway. I'm old enough to be your mother."

"You don't look it and you don't act it," he said brusquely. "How well did you know Red?"

She settled herself by the fire. "As well as anybody knew Red, I guess. How well did *you* know him?"

"Not very well," he admitted.

"He was hard," she said, "but he was fair. He took care of those he liked."

"I—it seems pretty hard to believe Red is dead," he said.

"Sure—the way you two had been so long."

He sat down across the fire from her, with a blanket on his shoulders. He felt impelled to talk about Red. "He was the fastest gunslinger of them all," he said. "Tallman couldn't have beaten him in a fair fight. It had to be murder. They drygulched him!"

"Maybe," she murmured, pulling her own blanket closer around her shoulders.

She was asleep in a minute.

The next morning he awoke at the first break of day-light in the east. It was cold, and Pearl had wrapped her-self in her blanket. He brought some wood and built up a fire, and she woke up, shaking her head and yawning. "Mighty hard beds in this hotel," she said, picking up her blanket. She shook it out and folded it, and did the same with his. He had staked both horses to be sure they wouldn't try to go back to Cripple Creek, and now he brought them in and saddled up.

"What's the next town?" asked Pearl.

"Silver City—a good day's ride."

"I could stand a cup of coffee," she said.

"With cream or without?" he asked.

She smiled at him. "Sure can't be much wrong with a man who can crack a joke this time of the morning," she said.

"Know anybody in Silver City?" he asked.

She nodded. "Sure do. Been up there to buy mining land options for your brother Red."

"How long is it since you saw him?" he asked.

"Quite a long time," she said, but he knew she was lying.

What was Pearl up to anyway? Had she been seeing Red on the sly? It didn't seem reasonable that a woman could carry on in such a small town, but then he remem-bered seeing Pearl leave on the stage and come back on the stage every once in a while. Come to think of it, that had been true ever since he had been in Cripple Creek, and he supposed now that either Duke didn't care or maybe she pretended to go on business all the time.

"It's gonna be hot today," he said as she pulled along-side him.

"I don't mind."

They jogged on for a while. "You say you've bought mining options in Silver City?"

"That's what I said, Johnny."

"Maybe we ought to go in business—if you know how it's handled and all."

"Suits me fine."

"You don't think Duke will come looking for us?"

"Not—not right away," she said.

"News travels pretty fast sometimes."

"And sometimes it doesn't. Silver City is a bigger town. We'll stay quiet for a while. I know some dealers. They're used to dealing with me—and they know me as Miss Jones."

"Miss Jones?" He nodded. "Good name."

"Good as any," she said.

Johnny's face was wrinkled up in a puzzled frown. "I never been where I had to make a living before. I just never thought about it. Red always told me what to do. It makes a man feel kind of—lost."

"How old are you, Johnny?"

"Twenty-three."

"Be glad you're not too old to learn, like old Pete Henderson. He'd starve to death if he had to go to work."

Johnny looked at her with new interest. "You really think so?"

"Sure," she said. "I know them all. Big words—little doin's. All kinds of advice for the other fellow to follow— but you don't catch them followin' any of it themselves, do you?"

"Hadn't thought about it," said Johnny.

"Look at Earl Tyler. He was starvin' to death when you run him for J. P. What is he now?"

"He isn't rich," said Johnny.

"He ain't starvin', either," Pearl pointed out.

The sun was coming up behind them, and the first rays were already lighting up the mountaintops to the north. A jack rabbit started up and made both horses shy, then disappeared among the bushes in long, zigzag jumps.

"We'll have to have water pretty soon," said Pearl.

"There's a spring off to the right about an hour farther on," he told her.

After a while they crossed a dry wash strewn with drift-wood from a flash flood, and presently a small gully, sandy-bottomed and dry. "This is where the stage crosses," he said. "Up here a way we'll find water."

They rode up the gully. Presently the sand showed signs of wetness, and a little later there were pools of water at intervals. They rounded a bend and came on an oasis of cottonwood trees around the spring. The water was cool and sweet. Johnny let the horses drink a little, pulled them back and rubbed them, let them drink again.

"If we had a gun of some kind," he said, "we might shoot a rabbit or even a deer. I see plenty of tracks around the spring."

"We haven't," she said, "and it's just as well. Guns get men into trouble."

He looked at her, puzzled. She was talking strange for a woman who had been in love with Red Concho—or was she?

"We'd better hit the trail," he said, "so we can pull into Silver City before dark."

They put their horses into a trot, and then another thought struck Johnny. "How can we buy options? I haven't got over ten dollars on me."

"How about what you won in the poker game last night?"

He hesitated, remembering some of the harsh things Tallman had said about that game. "It was all in chips," he recalled. "Anyway, I left it there when Tallman busted up the game."

"You don't have to worry about it," she told him. "I've still got the money I showed you, and that'll be enough for us to get started."

They rode into Silver City a little before sunset. It was a town of three thousand people—big enough to get lost in, Pearl pointed out, with a railroad running straight through from Albuquerque to Flagstaff, a spur up to the mountains, and several stagecoach lines. She guided him to the Withers Hotel. "The stagecoaches stop at the Hastings House," she said. "This is more out of the way."

They rented two rooms for a week, and Pearl paid for them with a gold piece.

"I sure don't like this," he said. "I never had a woman paying for me before."

She looked at him strangely. "Just call it interest on a debt I owe Red," she said, and went into her room.

Chapter Seven

THE NEXT MORNING he went with her to an office with a sign that said, "Ezra Smith. Mining Properties."

Ezra Smith was a shaky old man whose eyesight was so bad he had to hold a paper less than two inches from his nose to read it. He wore black sateen sleeve guards and red silk sleeve garters. "Miss Jones," he said. "Anything I can do for you today?"

"Want you to meet my partner, Johnny—Johnny Jones."

Ezra Smith looked at Johnny over his glasses. "Um— your brother, I take it. Pleased to make your acquaintance. Now, Miss Jones, what can I do for you?"

"What have you got in copper options?"

Ezra Smith began to putter at his desk. "Been some activity in options, Miss Jones. Quite a bit. Big strike up in the mountains last month, and everything is going up."

"I heard that," she said.

"Um—yes. Some of the options you bought from me last winter are worth several times what you paid—that is, if you want to sell."

"Pretty soon, maybe—not just yet."

"Don't pay to wait too long, you know. Sometimes a vein peters out and the option goes to nothing—though I must say it doesn't look that way up on Black Mountain."

"If you'd give me the locations," she said, "maybe we could tell better."

"Sure. Glad to. Here's a vertical map of the mountain and what's been found so far, and this shows the claims and legal locations."

"This will do fine," she said. "Just fine."

"Anything I can help you with," said Ezra, "let me know, ma'am. I not only buy and sell. I'm a broker too, you know—but best to let me know what you'd like. Some owners don't like to list their holdings. It affects the market."

"I know," said Pearl, examining the map.

"You'll be here all day?"

"Several days, most likely."

"Um—lots of activity, lots of activity. And you, young man. Anything special for you, or are you just—"

"I might," said Johnny, "look for a job." He saw Pearl's sharp glance in his direction. "Man has to earn a living," he said lamely.

"Most men do." The old man looked at Johnny over his glasses. "What are you suited for, young man?"

"Well, I—most anything, I reckon." Johnny hadn't thought this far ahead; he only knew vaguely that he couldn't live on Pearl's money. "What is there?"

"Lots of jobs, now the mines are opening up after the winter shutdown. Oh, Mr. Eccles!"

A tall, portly man wearing a silk hat and muttonchop whiskers that covered his collar, stopped at the door.

"Morning, Ezra!"

Ezra Smith hurried to the door, his frail legs taking short, quick steps. "Come in, Mr. Eccles. I may have— Miss Jones just came in—the lady who holds the option on that piece of property over the new vein you've uncovered."

Mr. Eccles was all smiles. He took off his silk hat with a flourish. "Miss Jones, it is indeed a pleasure to do business with such a charming young woman."

Pearl looked at him with a touch of warmth in her eyes, but her voice was casual. "We haven't done any business yet, Mr. Eccles."

Eccles laid his hat on Ezra Smith's desk. "Allow me to tell you who I am, Miss Jones. I'm chairman of the board of Arizona Amalgamated Mining and Investment. Now of course it is no secret that we have discovered a large deposit of copper in Black Mountain."

"So I heard," said Pearl.

"Mr. Smith here tells me that you hold a certain option to buy a mining claim under Arizona law which happens to lie over a vein we have opened up. You see I am being perfectly frank and honest with you, Miss Jones."

"So far," she said.

"We have explored this vein to a point which our engineers tell us is approximately under the edge of your option property, Miss Jones. Now, as you well realize, the vein might end within the next three feet, so there is no surety that copper will be found under your property. Likewise, I may remind you that the law is still not clearly defined in such cases as to who is entitled to the ore—the discoverer and exploiter or the legal owner of the title. Therefore I am prepared to make you a reasonable offer for your holding."

"If you aren't sure about the vein, Mr. Eccles, why are you prepared to settle?"

Johnny listened carefully. He had not suspected this side of Pearl Lang.

Mr. Eccles sighed. "The market, Miss Jones, the market. Raw copper is at a high level just now, and we can afford to pay you a neat profit on your holding so that we can go ahead and work the vein. This way both of us will make a profit."

"But if the land under my option turns out to be solid copper, then you stand to make a fortune."

Mr. Eccles shrugged. "Fortunes of business, Miss Jones. Love and war—you know about these things."

"On the other hand," Pearl said slowly, "if the vein plays out, then my option won't be worth the paper it's written on."

Mr. Eccles smiled. "You're a very astute young woman, Miss Jones—and I may add that your astuteness is matched only by your great loveliness."

She pretended not to be moved by that talk, but Johnny could see that she was pleased.

"Now, you paid," Mr. Eccles went on, "eighty dollars for that option, and we are prepared to make you a fair settlement. Say—"

"I hope," said Pearl, "you are not going to insult me."

Mr. Eccles held his hands palms up and shrugged. "You leave me no choice. You're a hard bargainer, young woman. What am I going to tell my board?"

"Tell them," she said coldly, "that you had to pay what this option is worth—and tell them it's worth it to get out of lawsuits and court costs."

"I take it you're about to ask some fantastic price."

"I wouldn't call it fantastic," said Pearl.

Mr. Eccles sighed. "Well, I am prepared to be extremely generous, young woman. By the way, that is a very becoming dress you are wearing."

Again she was pleased. She was wearing a skirt of plaid, an olive-green coat, and a dish-shaped hat on the back of her head. She flushed a little but said firmly, "The price, Mr. Eccles."

He put his hand to his chin and studied her. "Shall we say eight hundred dollars, Miss Jones?"

"You can say it," said Pearl, "but I'm not selling. That option is worth eight thousand if it's worth a peso."

"I'm afraid you're overestimating its value, Miss Jones."

"That's my price."

Eccles looked at her, his eyes clouded. He looked at the large cross section map of Black Mountain on the wall, at Ezra Smith, who shook his head with raised eyebrows, and at Johnny, who found all this completely over his head. "Well, in this one instance I might consider such a price," Eccles said at last, but added, "For one reason only, Miss Jones: the price of copper can very well go down and leave us both holding the bag, as you might say. I for one prefer to strike while the iron is hot—to get out the ore while the price is high. Eight thousand, then. Shall we settle it now?"

Johnny, watching Pearl, saw her falter, and knew something was wrong. "I haven't got the option in Silver City," she confessed.

Eccles's mouth turned down for a moment. "You hardly have anything to bargain with."

Pearl recovered from her confusion. "I have the option," she said, "and I'll have it here this week."

Eccles pursed his lips. "This week? I am afraid I cannot hold this offer open so long, Miss Jones. Let's say three days." He pulled a large gold watch from his vest pocket. "Seventy-two hours, to be exact. If you do not produce the option within that time, my offer is no good." He smiled. "It is obvious, Miss Jones, that you no longer have the option in your possession, but I will leave it up to you to obtain it. Good day, Miss Jones." He bowed rather stiffly. "Mr. Smith. Mr. Jones. Good day."

He was gone in a flourish of coattails.

Ezra Smith looked at Pearl, nodding slowly. "You run a considerable bluff," he said. "Do you think you can get the option back?"

"For eight thousand dollars," she said fiercely, "I could get an option to the whole of Arizona Territory."

"Three days," Ezra Smith said. "Seventy-two hours."

She looked at him without seeing him. "I'll have it," she said.

"Tricky business—options," said Ezra Smith. "Fortunes are made and lost in a day—and more are lost than are made. It's like most businesses, Miss Jones. Time is of the essence. What is worth a great deal today will be valueless tomorrow—and for just the reason Mr. Eccles mentioned —the market. If copper drops three cents a pound, then it won't be economical to mine Black Mountain, no matter how rich the vein is. It costs too much to get the ore and smelt it and ship it east."

"They should be smelting it at the mine," she said.

"Time," he said on an exhaled breath. "Time is every-thing. It takes not only money but several months to buy machinery and get it shipped out here and set up. In the meantime, things change, and no company will make a big investment in equipment when they cannot even be sure of control of the mineral rights. Black Mountain originally was prospected pretty thoroughly by individ-uals, and a lot of claims were registered, so you can hardly blame Amalgamated for trying to get control." He looked at her over his glasses. "Regardless of what they have found under your claim, or what they think they have found, he made a very generous offer, Miss Jones, and I advise—"

"I'll be back," she said impatiently, "three days from now—with the option."

Ezra Smith nodded. "Don't forget, Miss Jones, an option is short-lived."

"I know." She nodded. "The option is about a month old. There's plenty of time—but I'll have it here, Mr. Smith."

"Eight thousand dollars!" he said to himself. "A young fortune!"

Pearl and Johnny went outside. "Let's go get some-thing to eat," she said. "I'm hungry."

They went into a restaurant. It was after eight o'clock, and the tables were mostly empty. A couple of miners sat at the counter and gave Pearl close scrutiny. It made

Johnny rather proud, for she was a good-looking woman, and this morning, after a night's sleep, she didn't look her age at all.

They sat at a table, and a waiter came up with his apron thrown over his shoulder. "Ham and eggs," he said, "or pancakes."

"Ham and," said Pearl.

"Me too," said Johnny.

She tried the water and made an unpretty face. "Cripple Creek's whisky is better than this."

He said curiously, "I don't think I ever saw you drink whisky."

She glanced up at him. "I've tasted it," she said quickly. "Enough to know what it's like."

Johnny said, his brow wrinkled: "All that about options and all—I don't think I'd ever understand that."

"Neither did Red," she said. "That's why he had me handle it."

"I can't make head nor tail of it."

"You'll get used to it."

"Not me," he declared. "I need something I can see, like—" He had started to say poker, but now, remembering the kind of game he had played in Cripple Creek, he changed it. "Like driving a team or something."

Her voice was almost scornful. "You couldn't drive a team. Your hands are too soft."

"They'll get tough," he said, looking at them.

"Johnny, you've never worked in your life, have you?"

"I never had to. I never thought about it."

"Well, you don't have to start thinking now." She put a hand on his arm. "I told you I'd take care of you, and I mean it, Johnny. I've got money, and there'll be more— plenty more."

"What do I do?" asked Johnny.

"Nothing—just what you did in Cripple Creek."

He looked at her. "You think—that's all right—to do nothing?"

"Only the dumb ones work," she assured him.

He shook his head. "I never had a woman pay my way."

She seemed almost anxious. "You'll get used to it. Now I'll tell you what we'll do after breakfast. You go around and see about the horses, and I'll look up some brokers and see how the market's going."

"I thought that was why you saw Ezra Smith."

"He's only one," she said. "The others may have a different story."

She was indeed a smart woman—far smarter than he had ever suspected. He nodded.

"And another thing—go to the post office and ask for mail."

"For me? Nobody in Cripple Creek would write to me—unless—" He was thinking of Mary.

"Do what I say," she told him. "You never know."

They had breakfast, and she reached for the bag of gold in her bosom.

"No," said Johnny. "I'm paying for the breakfast."

"Don't be foolish," she said, opening the bag. "Your money won't last a day if you start paying."

Johnny pulled two silver dollars out of his pocket. "I'm paying for this," he said.

She looked at him contemplatively. "Okay, Johnny." She put her slim hand on his arm. "Whatever you say."

He got back his change and put it in his pocket.

"Now I'll pay for the horses," she said. "You can pay me back later if you're determined to."

He didn't have much choice. He took the gold piece and went to the Black Mountain Stable around the corner. He went into the office but nobody was inside. He went on through and stepped down into the corral, sour with horse and sweet with the smell of opened hay. A man was forking straw from a runway over the stalls, and Johnny waited until he got down. "I want to leave some money for those two horses," he said. "The bay and the sorrel."

"Pay at the end of the wee—" The man looked closely at him. "You come in with a woman last night from the east?"

"Yes."

"From Cripple Creek, maybe."

"Yes."

"Heard there was some trouble in Cripple Creek."

"Some."

"You Johnny Concho, by any chance?"

"Yes. Red Concho's brother."

"Red is dead, I hear."

"I heard that," Johnny said steadily.

"And I heard his killer took over Cripple Creek."

Johnny didn't answer. The liveryman squinted at him. "Second thought, maybe you *better* leave me some money on them animals' keep. Man like you is here today and gone tomorrow."

"That's what I came here for," Johnny said stiffly.

"I'll give you a receipt." The man went into the office to write it out. "Town's growing," he said at last. "Full of miners and strangers. You can't trust people the way you used to." He handed the receipt to Johnny.

Johnny put the slip in his pocket and inquired the way to the post office. He found the general delivery window and stepped into line with a dozen high-booted, roughly dressed men from the mines. "Johnny Concho," he said when his turn came.

The man at the window looked up from under his green eyeshade. "Johnny Concho? Come from Cripple Creek?"

"Yes," Johnny said.

"Had a fight or something, didn't you?"

"I came for mail," Johnny said harshly.

"Oh, sure. Just curious." He made no effort to look for mail. "Heard you got faced down by the man killed your brother."

Johnny said harshly, "I want my mail."

The men leaned halfway through the window. "Heard you didn't even draw."

Johnny said in a tight voice, "You want me to come through this window after you?"

"Just a minute." The man backed away. Then suddenly the window slammed down in Johnny's face. He stared at it a moment, took a deep breath, and turned away. One of the miners in the line behind him said, "It don't look like the Concho brothers are doin' so good any more."

Chapter Eight

JOHNNY WENT BACK to the hotel. Pearl was sitting in a chair downstairs, looking over some papers. "I picked up a few options this morning," she said. "How about you? Any luck at the post office?"

"Uh—no," he said. He had been insulted enough without telling about it.

"You're sure?" she asked.

He looked at her, not understanding why she was so insistent. "I didn't get any," he said.

"Well—maybe tomorrow."

"I've got to do something," he said, "to make some money."

"I thought I told you—"

"I know what you told me," he said impatiently, "but I want some money of my own. I never depended on a woman for money."

"Johnny—"

"Shut up!" he said.

Presently she asked, considerably chastened, by the sound of her voice, "What will you do, Johnny?"

"The only thing I know—poker."

"Johnny! Do you think you can—I mean—"

"Say it!" he ordered. "Say what you're thinking. Say that we weren't playing poker in Cripple Creek. Sure, I know that. I know it as well as anybody. But I can play poker. I grew up with a deck of cards in my hands. Red taught me how to play—and I did all right with it before I ever heard of Cripple Creek!"

She said soothingly, "All right, Johnny. I didn't know. I guess you've got more of Red in you than anybody thought." She nodded. "I don't want you to be mad at me, Johnny," she pleaded. "If you want to play poker, I'll back you."

"Lend me fifty!" he said abruptly.

"Yes, Johnny."

She opened the coin pouch. "You sure fifty is enough?"

"It's enough," he said, taking two double eagles and

72

a ten-dollar gold piece. He got up. "I'll see you after while. If I'm late, don't worry. I might get into a good winning streak—and if I do," he said fiercely, "I'll make enough in one game to buy the whole town of Silver City."

She held out her hand toward him as he stood up. "Be careful, Johnny."

He nodded, pulled his hat down harder, and left. He stopped in at the first saloon he came to and had a shot of whisky. "Any action around here?" he asked.

"Depends," said the bartender.

"On what?"

"How high you want to go."

"Not too high," said Johnny. "Not right away."

The bartender nodded toward a table across the room. "Little game there. They might need another hand."

There were only four men playing, and from their looks three of them were miners; one was a rancher. One of the miners wore a better hat than the others. "Mind if I sit in?" asked Johnny.

The man with the good hat looked up. "Not at all. Pull up a chair, mister. My name's Blixen."

Johnny sat down. "What's the limit?"

"Table stakes; dealer names his own limit. Not over five dollars on a bet. We ain't rich, like old man Eccles." He guffawed.

"I'm Yates," said the second man.

The one who looked like a rancher glanced up and said, "Rutledge, Bar Seven Bar out south of town."

The third man grunted.

"He's deaf and dumb," said Blixen. "Name is Farrington."

They all looked expectantly at Johnny.

"Call me Johnny." He counted out forty dollars. "You're using money, I see."

"Sure. Chips come from the East, and they cost too damn' much. Gold and silver don't wear out. That's hard money and this is a hard-money country. What do you say, Farrington?"

Farrington looked up, saw that something was expected of him, grunted, and looked around at them all, well pleased with their smiles.

"Ante two bits," said Blixen, who was about to deal.

Johnny got change. With a dollar and a quarter in the pot as openers, Blixen let Johnny cut the cards and began to deal.

"From around here?" Rutledge asked Johnny.

"No."

"Face is familiar—or maybe it's your name."

Johnny's voice was cutting. "I said not from around here."

Rutledge studied him, his eyes narrow. "All right, Johnny. All right."

Johnny picked up his cards. He had an ace and four small cards.

"Your open," said Blixen.

"What's the limit again?"

"Five. Always five unless somebody changes it. There's no limit on the draw. You open?"

Johnny slid out a gold half-eagle the size of a penny. "Five," he said.

Blixen raised his eyebrows. "Man's got a hand." He looked at his cards. "I'll stay this round."

Yates frowned and shook his head, tossed in his cards.

Rutledge, the rancher, scowled as he pushed in five silver dollars. "Price of a heifer these days," he said.

Farrington looked up quickly, looked at Johnny and held up four fingers and a thumb, with his eyebrows raised. Johnny nodded, and Farrington's lower lip protruded as he considered. Then he tossed away two cards and pushed in five dollars.

"Cards?" said Blixen.

"Gimme one," said Rutledge.

The single card floated over the table. "Most likely sitting on two pair," said Blixen, "*or* a possible straight or flush. Help you any, Rutledge?"

"Maybe," said the rancher, and put the card in his hand without looking at it.

Blixen drummed on the table with his knuckles, and Farrington looked up, eyebrows high. He raised two fingers.

"Bobtailed straight, most likely," said Blixen, "but he could have threes."

"Four," said Johnny, throwing away his small cards. "Proud of the big ace, eh?" He floated four cards onto the table in front of Johnny. "I'll take four myself," he said. "See if I can match up my ace in case you didn't."

Johnny paid no attention to this talk, for he knew it meant nothing. Every man there could figure pretty close to what every other man had. The difference between "pretty close" and "exactly" was the dividing line between winning and losing.

"You opened," said Blixen.

"I like my aces," said Johnny. "Five dollars."

He had not picked up his cards. Neither had Blixen. "I like my pair," said Blixen. "I'll stay."

Rutledge pushed out an eagle. "Raise you five," he said. Farrington called.

Johnny still hadn't looked, but he felt his luck was good. "That, and five more," he said.

"Whoa!" said Blixen. "Man doesn't look at his cards, bets on a lone ace. Mighty big ace—but not that big. If you can bet, I can stay."

"Five more," said Rutledge.

Farrington was watching. Now he held up both hands.

Blixen said, "Another country heard from! The dummy must have filled."

Johnny picked up his draw-cards and saw an ace and three sixes. He laid it down again. "And five," he said.

Blixen seemed to shiver. He picked up his own hand, glanced at it, and said, "And five of my own."

Rutledge looked at them both and then at his hand. "I'll pry that once more," he said.

Farrington frowned exaggeratedly. Finally he shook his head and tossed out a double eagle.

Blixen grunted as if he had been hit.

Johnny now had $30 in the pot, and it would cost him ten more to see the last two raises. He glanced at his cards again to be sure. Then he pushed out the $5 piece in front of him, and dug the last $10 Pearl had given him out of his pocket. "I'm raising five," he said.

Blixen studied his cards for a moment. "Can't quit now," he said.

Rutledge now looked at his one draw-card for the first time, and Johnny knew he had drawn to two pairs. He looked up. "I'm going to raise five," he said. "You've already got into your pockets," he told Johnny, "and you don't have to call unless you want to. This can be a side bet."

Farrington looked at each one in turn. Blixen held up ten fingers, and Farrington nodded slowly, pushed out a gold piece, and closed his cards together and waited.

"You did have openers, didn't you?" asked Blixen.

Johnny looked up suddenly. "Huh? Oh, sure."

"Takes jacks or better, you know."

"Yes, sure." He hadn't known, but he wasn't going to start worrying about it now, with over $200 in the pot.

Blixen called.

Farrington laid out his hand and smiled.

"A nice hand," said Blixen. "An eight-high straight."

"But not good enough for me. Mine's ten high." He laid them out.

There was now $221 on the table, and Johnny looked at Rutledge. The man probably had matched one of his pairs—but which one?

Rutledge turned them over one at a time. Two kings and three deuces.

Johnny drew a deep breath. "A good hand," he said. "Worth a herd of cows—sometimes." He laid down his two aces and three sixes and reached for the money.

There was quite an audience around them, very quiet.

But he felt a hand on his wrist. It was Farrington, the dummy, and he held up two fingers.

"Wants to see your openers," said Blixen. "Rules of the game, of course." He frowned and looked at Johnny. "You kept an ace," he said. "If you had a pair of jacks or better, why didn't you draw to them?" He looked sharply at Johnny. "What *did* you throw away?"

"I—" Johnny stared at them. Farrington's hand was still on his wrist. Rutledge was scowling at him. Blixen looked suspicious. Suddenly Johnny was desperate. All of his money was on the table—and enough more to make him independent of Pearl. He shouted, "Turn loose of me!"

But Farrington just looked at him with his eyebrows raised high.

Blixen said, "They must be in the discard. What did you have, anyway, Johnny?"

A familiar figure stepped up to the table at the side

of Rutledge. Johnny saw the batwing collar and Prince Albert coat—Pearson, the man from the East. "I've seen this man play poker before," he said. "In Cripple Creek!"

"Cripple Creek?" Blixen looked at Pearson and at Benson just behind him. "You gents were in Cripple Creek? You know this man?"

Pearson nodded emphatically. "Sure, we saw him run out of Cripple Creek for cheatin' at cards. He called three queens when he had only two."

"Is it so?" asked Blixen.

Johnny tried to control himself. He could have got out of this if the damned Easterners had kept still. "Shut up!" he shouted.

"Now wait a minute," said Blixen. "A thing like this needs lookin' into. Maybe it was a mistake."

Johnny stared at him helplessly. "It *was* a mistake," he muttered.

"All right, now. One thing at a time. Let's get at the openers. Was that a mistake too?"

"It's my money," said Johnny. "I put my own money in there."

"When you open, you can't take the pot without openers," said Blixen irrevocably.

"Damn you!" Johnny said to Pearson.

Pearson lunged across the table at him, and Johnny leaped to his feet. The table went over; cards scattered and gold coins rolled over the floor. Johnny tried to get to Pearson, but they were holding him from behind. He struck and flailed blindly, but hit nothing.

When he finally cooled off, he saw Blixen sitting on the floor examining the cards. "I still can't find your openers," he said. "There ain't a pair of anything higher than tens in the whole discard!"

Chapter Nine

JOHNNY WAS DEJECTED that day at dinner. "Everything I ever did," he said, "has followed me here. I think we ought to go farther west."

"Johnny," Pearl said, "those things don't ever quit following you. The world isn't big enough."

"But I never did anything in Cripple Creek," he cried. "I never hurt anybody. I did what Red told me to do. I chased the gunslingers out of town like Red said, and Cripple Creek paid me for it."

"Men like Pearson and Benson," she observed, "don't understand all that. Easterners!"

"I thought," he said, "I'd found something I could do."

She put a hand on his arm. "Don't worry, Johnny. I made sixty-five dollars selling options today."

"That doesn't help me."

"You're gettin' mighty fussy for a man who—"

"A man who what?" he asked quickly.

"Never mind, never mind. The main thing is—how much did you lose today?"

"Too much."

"Here's forty more."

"I don't need it," he said firmly. "It's not that I'm short of money. I just don't like everybody landing on me."

"They been doin' that pretty regular," she noted.

"Listen, Pearl! I'm going to get a job. I'm going to work."

She sighed. "If you gotta, you gotta."

"I don't know why, but I want to."

"Where'll you start lookin'?"

"Anywhere. Anywhere to get away from those damned Easterners! They had no business stickin' their noses in!"

She looked at him. "All right, Johnny. Only don't give up your room at the hotel, will you? I'll be afraid unless I know you're around."

"Afraid!" He said scornfully, "I can't even take care of myself, let alone somebody else."

"It won't always be that way, Johnny."

He stood up. "Maybe," he said. "And maybe Johnny Concho is as no-good as some people think."

He went to the railroad depot to ask about a job.

"Plenty of jobs around Silver City," said the station agent. "Where you from?"

"East."

"What can you do?"

"Anything."

"Ever do any railroad work?"

"No."

"I reckon that lets 'anything' out, then. Drive a team?"

"Sure."

"Go down to the Amalgamated Corral and ask for the freighter foreman."

"Thanks," said Johnny.

Silver City was a busy town. The dirt in the street was constantly churned and rechurned to a fine powder; little wagons and big freight wagons went through one after another, headed to and coming from the mountains. Saddle horses stood at every hitching-rail. Saloons were filled with men, and mechanical bands blared music into every street.

He found the Amalgamated Corral, a huge place with dozens of big wagons and hundreds of mules and horses. He asked for the foreman, and was told, "In there." He went into the office on the corner. A man sat behind a paper with his feet in the window sill.

"I'm looking for the foreman," said Johnny.

The paper came down, and he was facing Blixen. He got set and clenched his fists, but Blixen unexpectedly said, "Take it easy, sonny. I've got nothing against you."

"Yes, but—"

Blixen shook his head sadly. "I was tryin' to find a pair for you so you could take the pot. You looked to me like you needed to win."

"But Farrington—"

"He didn't mean anything. It's the way we play, that's all. If Farrington had really known you didn't have openers, he probably would of been too scared to do anything about it."

"Then you weren't—layin' for me."

Blixen put down his paper. "Listen, Johnny Concho, I got nothin' against you. Sure, I heard them blankety-blank Easterners shoot off their mouths—but what does that mean? Did you ever see an Easterner that wouldn't open his mouth and forget to close it? Now look, Johnny, I don't know what went on in Cripple Creek and I don't figure it's any of my business. I need drivers. If you can drive, you've got a job. Only come clean and tell me how much you can drive."

"I've been around ranches and ranch towns all my life," said Johnny. "I never had a job driving, but I can handle six mules without any trouble."

"Mighty soft hands you got."

Johnny said harshly, "I told you I never drove for a living."

"That's right, you did. Tell you what—" He got out of the caboose chair and went to the window. "There's Farrington hitching up a team now. It'll be an empty wagon going up to Black Mountain, but you'll come back with a load. Think you can make it?"

"Sure," said Johnny.

Blixen looked at him. "You lost everything you had in that game, didn't you?"

"Almost," said Johnny.

"Here's three dollars. Go buy yourself a pair of horse-hide gloves. You'll need 'em. Come back here and your team will be ready."

Johnny took the money.

"By the way, you didn't need to get so excited about that pot. You wouldn't have lost your money, you know. We would of given you your money back—but we couldn't let you win. You know that, don't you?"

Johnny nodded.

"Maybe they play different rules in Cripple Creek," Blixen said, "but that's the way we play here."

Johnny found a general store a block away, and went in and picked out a pair of horse-hide gloves. He put them on and stretched his fingers. The gloves made him feel proud, the way he had over the new pants back in the third grade. He went to the hotel and told Pearl. She nodded, watching his eyes. "Maybe I better call for your mail, since you won't be here," she said.

"There won't be any mail," said Johnny.

"You never can tell."

"There's nobody to write me."

Pearl shrugged.

He started away, but she called him back. "Johnny, you'll need some eatin' money." She opened the pouch. "Here's ten."

"I won't need it," said Johnny. "I've got a job."

"If you don't eat, you won't be able to keep the job. Take it, Johnny, for Red's sake."

"Red?" he said. "Yes, I guess so. That's the way Red would do it." He took the gold piece and put it in his pocket.

Back at the corral he found the wagon ready. Farrington made rapid signs with his hands, and Blixen spoke up behind him. "He's trying to tell you he's sorry for gettin' you into trouble."

"That's all right," said Johnny. "I had it comin', I guess."

"Now you follow out the street here and take the road up to Black Mountain. You'll see a sign up there that says, 'Dispatcher.' Stop your team there and McDonald will tell you what to do. All set?"

"Yes."

"Let's see if you can take them out of the yard."

Johnny climbed into the seat and unwound the six reins from around the seat iron. He got them distributed, one line between two fingers. The lines came in over his index fingers, and the end trailed on the floor of the wagon.

"You can hold the reins, anyhow," said Blixen.

Johnny braced his feet and slapped the reins on the mules' backs and shouted: "Hieieiii!" The team moved off through the gate, and Blixen shouted, "Good luck!"

He had no trouble getting the wagon on the road, and the mules were used to harness, so he made the fifteen miles to the mountain in good time. Then the road went up a long grade, and began a series of curves and climbs, and presently it narrowed to the width of one wagon.

He hit a level stretch and took off his gloves and saw that his hands were red and tender. He put the gloves back on and took the team up the mountain to the dispatcher's office. He gave his name and waited.

"Johnny Concho!" McDonald said. "Never expected to see you drivin' a team for Amalgamated."

"What *did* you expect to see?" Johnny asked coldly.

"Well, I—" McDonald looked at his face. "Nothing, I guess."

"Then keep your mouth shut," said Johnny. "You're not paid for what you expect."

McDonald looked at him, and his eyes slowly narrowed. He looked at Johnny's waist, and Johnny knew he was looking for a gun.

"Ever drive a jerkline team?" he asked.

"No."

"You'll take back an ore train—three wagons, eighteen mules."

"I told you I never drove a jerkline."

"You hired out as a mule skinner, didn't you?"

"Yes."

"You're nothin' but a name on the payroll to me," McDonald said. "It happens I need a jerkline driver to take an ore train back to Silver City. Do you want the job or don't you?"

"Sure I want the job!"

"All right. Leave this team here. There's a train loading up on the dump there. Report to Bob Williams and tell him I said to give you the best team we've got."

Johnny compressed his lips. "All right. I'll try."

"Get going!"

Johnny frowned. Then he started on foot up the slope. Nothing but a mule could have found footing up there. He took off his gloves and rubbed his hands. They'd be plenty sore tomorrow. He grinned. Tomorrow was another day. He'd make a stake driving, and then he'd have another shot at poker. Maybe this time he could remember the rules. He'd been playing by his own rules so long he'd almost forgotten.

Williams was a big, black-bearded man with eyes like an eagle's. He watched Johnny as Johnny reported, and glanced at Johnny's hands. "Best team we've got," he repeated. "You'll get it, mister."

Half a dozen men were shoveling blue-hued copper carbonate into the three wagons—the first a huge one, the second smaller and trailing the first one with its tongue fastened to the rear axle of the first one, and the third still smaller and fastened the same way. Johnny felt a little scared when he saw that, for there would be maybe 30,000 pounds of ore in those wagons. And eighteen mules in a jerkline string down the mountain!

The hostlers were bringing out the mules now and placing them along the big chain. "You might as well go in and have some coffee and a piece of pie," one of them said to Johnny. "We'll be half an hour yet."

Johnny nodded and went into the cookshack. The cook twirled a heavy china cup of steaming coffee under his nose and said, "Name it, mister."

"Apple pie."

"On the house."

He put the gloves in his hip pocket and picked up the coffee to blow on it. Then Williams came into the cookshack and roared: "You, there!"

"Yeah?" said Johnny.

Williams stamped over to him and jerked the gloves out of his pocket. "What's the idea, trying to swipe McDonald's gloves?"

Johnny was up instantly. "Those are my gloves!" he said.

"That ain't the way I heard it from McDonald, sonny."

"McDonald lied!"

"I wouldn't say that if I was you."

"I said he lied!"

"Are you accusin' *me* of bein' a liar?"

"I said McDonald lied."

"Maybe you got some way of provin' it."

"I don't have to prove it. I want my gloves."

"Can you take 'em away from me?"

Johnny launched himself at the big man. It was like hitting a stone wall. The big man laughed and pushed him with a huge arm that sent him back against the end of the cookshack. Johnny couldn't find his feet until he was on the floor.

"You're Johnny Concho, ain't you?" said Williams. "You got smart with McDonald. That ain't healthy."

Johnny got ready to leap at him.

"Don't try it!" Williams said suddenly. "I've broken the back of better men than you for even thinking about it."

Johnny got to his feet. "Those are my gloves," he insisted.

"Not while I've got them."

Johnny started blindly outside.

"Here's your pie!" shouted the cook.

"Feed it to the coyotes!" Johnny growled, and went out.

It scared him when he contemplated the string of ore wagons. The pairs of mules fastened to the chain made a team over a hundred feet long, and the wagons coming behind added another fifty or sixty. It was like driving a freight train through the mountains without any tracks to keep it in place.

As driver, he would ride the near wheel-mule and handle two long reins that went through rings on each mule's pair of hames to the front pair of mules, and he would have a helper on each wagon to handle the brake. Williams came and handed him a coiled blacksnake whip. "Understand your brother was good with a whip," he said. "I always intended to try him out some time."

Johnny nodded. His words were sarcastic. "A lot of people intended to try Red out but never got around to it—and I'll tell you why!" he shouted suddenly. "Because they didn't have the guts to face him!"

Williams's weathered face reddened. "You ain't got his guns behind you now," he said, but he wasn't too sure of himself.

Johnny pressed his advantage. "I don't need them," he said. "You'll all eat crow before this is over—I promise!"

"Promises don't mean much in the mountains," said Williams. "You deliver the goods—that's all that counts."

"Your mules are ready, Johnny Concho!"

"Take this team to the Santa Fe loading dock," said Williams, "and report to Blixen for another wagon out."

"Do I get my gloves?" Johnny demanded.

"You'll get 'em!" Williams slapped him across the face with them.

Johnny launched into him headfirst. Williams gasped as it got him in the pit of his stomach, and bent over while he tried to get his feet under him. Then he stepped off the edge of the dock and fell into a pile of ore. He came up with his face bleeding. "Johnny Concho!" he roared, and came in fighting.

It was short and bloody. Johnny found himself on his back in a pile of ore, the jagged edges cutting into his flesh. His face was bloody and his nose felt much too big. He saw Williams waiting for him at the edge of the dock.

Johnny got up slowly and went to the wheel-horse. He got into the saddle and took the lines and the whip. He let out a rolling "Hieieieiii!" and cracked the whip over the heads of the mules. He pulled on the left rein, and the head of the long team turned in a great circle to get back to the road, their bells jingling a warning to another team approaching them on the one-way road.

Grimly he got them straightened out, and began to breathe more easily. He'd have a pair of sore hands when he pulled into Silver City, but he'd bring the ore in just the same.

They hit the first downgrade, and the helpers on the wagons rared back on the brakes. The mules kept following the road, their bells jingling. They came to the first sharp turn, and it went all right. They went through a dip and up the other side and around another sharp turn. That was where he got into trouble.

As the first several spans of mules put their necks into the collars, the long chain straightened out. The lead mules went out of sight around the curve, and the middle span of mules was pulled over against the cliff. The near mule, scraped along the jagged rocks, let out a snort and stampeded. He climbed over the chain and across the back of the mule diagonally ahead of him. That one trumpeted a scream of fear and tried to break out of his harness. The whole team surged to the right. The lead mules were jerked off of their feet, and one, struggling to get back up, fell over the edge. Then the entire team went over, one mule at a time, one span at a time, pulled down by the heavy weight of the mules dangling from the chain below.

The cliff was two hundred feet high, and as Johnny watched in horror, the helper in the first wagon shouted: "Jump!" and left the wagon on the near side. Johnny left the saddle as the wheel mules were dragged off the road. The lead wagon tottered for a moment; then its right front wheel went over the edge, and in a few seconds, with a great, slow creaking of boards and the screech of chains, the entire train went into the ravine.

Johnny stood there shaking his head. "I told him I wasn't a jerkline driver," he said. "Somebody go back and get Williams. A lot of these mules will have to be shot."

"Where are *you* going, Johnny Concho?"

Johnny pulled his hat tight on his head. He looked at his hands, now covered with big blisters. "Back to Silver City," he said bitterly, "to see what else they can dish out."

Chapter Ten

JOHNNY SAW wagons coming, and took to the mountains where they could not follow him except on foot. He heard distant shots, and knew they were killing the mules. He stayed above the road and tried to follow the ridge. And about dark he got out of the mountains and started across the desert toward the town.

He reached it the next morning about daylight, and went to the hotel. He got to his room and washed his face. He heard a soft knock and said, "Come in."

Pearl entered, her face filled with apprehension. She looked at Johnny and gave a little scream. "What did they do to you?"

"I just got tangled up with some mules," he told her.

"When you didn't get back for supper, I asked about you, and finally this Mr. Blixen told me you'd taken a team to the copper mines."

"Yup."

"Sit down, Johnny. I'll go to the kitchen and get some warm water for your face."

He sat down. He had to admit it was nice to have somebody look after him—and Pearl, at that. She was a good-looking woman even at this hour of the morning.

She came back with a pan of warm water and a soft cloth. She made him lie on the bed while she cleansed his face. She discovered the blisters on his hands and whispered, "Oh, Johnny!"

And Johnny mumbled, "You shoulda seen Williams when he was climbing out of that ore."

"Johnny, you can't keep on like this."

"I don't know how to do anything else," he said honestly. "I go around minding my own business and trying to make a living—and everybody ups and takes a crack at me. All because I'm Johnny Concho!"

"Or because you're Red Concho's brother," she said, "and they expect you to be something you are not."

"They damn sure better watch out," he said. "I never had to look out for myself before, and I was soft, and I

87

didn't know how mean people could be—but I'm learnin'.
I'm learnin' fast."

"Don't try too hard, Johnny."

"Some day," he said grimly, "they'll find out Johnny
Concho is just as much dynamite as Red Concho was."

"Johnny, is that what you want?"

"How else can I live?" he demanded, sitting up. "They
drygulch me every time I turn around. What else can I
do but fight back?"

"I don't want you to do that, Johnny. Red was like that.
He was hard—terribly hard. Too hard to live. That's why
he died."

"There's no reason why I can't be as hard as he was.
It may take me a little while to learn, but they're teachin'
me fast."

"You can't be hard unless it's in you, Johnny—and I
don't think it is."

"Are you askin' me to live the rest of my days under
the heel of every man who hears my name?"

"Shhh—not so loud, Johnny." She shook her head. "I
don't know; but there must be other ways."

"It doesn't look like it. You're either hard or you get
kicked around by everybody."

"I don't know, Johnny. My parents were killed by
Apaches, and I've had to get along the best I could too.
It's different for a woman. A man fights it out; a woman
smiles her way out. But maybe there's a different way for
both. I don't know, and I don't guess I'll live long enough
to find out."

Johnny took the towel to dry his face. "I aim to live
a long time," he said. "And I aim to find the answers."

He slept a while. Pearl awoke him and they had breakfast. He let her pay for it, and that reminded him of Blixen.
He owed Blixen three dollars.

In the afternoon he went around to the Amalgamated
Corral and found Blixen.

"I heard you had a run-in with McDonald," Blixen
said, "and that you deliberately ran eighteen mules and
three wagons off the road and down the side of the mountain."

"You know damn well you heard wrong," Johnny said.
"I told you when I hired out that I could drive a six-mule

team, and that's why you put me on the road with it."

"Then why did you start back with a jerkline?"

"Because McDonald ordered me to."

"Didn't you—"

"Just as plain as I'm tellin' you now: I never drove a jerkline team. But he never left me any argument."

Blixen sat back. "They saved three of them mules. Mules are worth a lot of money up here—three or four hundred apiece. Wagons are worth a lot too."

"I did my damnedest," said Johnny.

"Let's see your hands, Johnny."

"They were tender," Johnny said.

"What happened to your gloves?"

"I lost 'em."

"To McDonald?"

"Back in the mountains," said Johnny.

"I saw you wearin' them gloves," said Blixen, "and I said to myself, 'There's a young fellow mighty proud because he's wearin' something he's earning himself.' So I don't figure you lost them in the mountains, Johnny."

"It doesn't make any difference," Johnny said. "They're gone."

Blixen nodded. "I don't reckon you want to try the Black Mountain run again."

"No. I come to tell you I owe you for the gloves and I'll pay you—when I get it."

"What are you goin' to do now?"

"How the hell do I know?" asked Johnny. "What *can* I do?"

"Keep tryin'," Blixen said slowly. "Keep tryin'. Maybe you'll wear 'em out."

Johnny went back to the hotel. Pearl said, "You better go ask for your mail, Johnny."

He stared at her. "Why do you keep wanting me to ask for mail?"

She was wide-eyed—too wide-eyed, he thought. "Everybody asks for mail."

"I told you there's nobody to write to me. Red is gone, and nobody—"

"Wouldn't Mary Dark write you?"

"When she thinks I ran off with you?"

"Well, anyway," she said, "you'd better ask."

"The post office clerk slammed the window in my face yesterday."

"That was yesterday, Johnny. He can't do that every day."

"I been hearin' about a lot of things people can't do, but they keep right on doin' them."

"Now listen: I'm going over to Ezra Smith. You go to the post office and meet me at Smith's place. We'll have something to eat and talk it over."

He thought about Mary as he went alone to the post office. After the hectic events that made Tallman's first appearance in Cripple Creek seem years ago, Mary was very real to him. He could see her black hair, her clear skin, her neat apron; he could hear her soft voice and feel her lips against his. And suddenly he was homesick and he wanted to see Mary, but in the same moment he realized he could not, for nothing had changed. Tallman was still in Cripple Creek and he would shoot Johnny on sight, and Johnny didn't know how to use a gun and didn't have the confidence to try. Maybe some people called it just plain crawfishing—and maybe it was.

He stepped to the window and asked again for mail for Johnny Concho. This time the man glared at him but he ran through a handful of letters and said, "Nope, not today."

Johnny turned away. For a moment he had hoped there might be a letter from Mary, but now he knew it was foolish to think a thing like that. The town of Cripple Creek knew by now that Johnny and Pearl had gone away together, and he knew Mary had too much pride to interfere.

He walked back toward Ezra Smith's place, and passed the Hastings House where the stagecoaches arrived. He paid no notice to the passengers sitting there until he heard a voice call, "Johnny Concho!"

He turned and saw Mrs. Brown's sharp features. "How do, Mrs. Brown," he said.

"Do sit down," she said. "I never was so pleased to see anybody in my whole life."

He sat down. "Why should you be pleased to see me, Mrs. Brown?"

"I always liked you, young man. You were arrogant and bossy but you never did any real harm—and I thought it was disgraceful the way the people allowed Tallman to run you out of town."

"Yes'm."

"I told my husband Hez when he got home that night—I think it's a public scandal the way they let that stranger take over Cripple Creek. And Hez just grunted and said it was good riddance, but I don't hold with that. No, sir, it is my belief that every person fulfills a purpose, and the Lord must have had a purpose in mind when He brought you to Cripple Creek, Johnny Concho."

"If He did," said Johnny, "He seems to have let it slip His mind."

"Well," she said, "if they thought things were bad before—they are twice as bad now. Tallman and Walker are laying a twenty per cent tax on everything. You should hear Joe Helgeson complain!"

"But nobody does anything?"

"Not so you could notice. I asked Hez, I said, 'What have we got a sheriff for? Isn't he supposed to handle cases like this?' But Hez just grunted and said he guessed the sheriff knows his own business. What do *you* think, Johnny Concho?"

"I'll tell you the truth, Mrs. Brown. I got so many things to think about I don't know where to begin."

"I saw Mary yesterday," she said. "She's as sweet as ever—and looking very lonely."

Johnny nodded.

"They say her father and mother are worried about her. She seems so sad—and that's not good for a young woman her age. Do you think so, Johnny?"

He didn't answer. There was no need.

"There's talk," she whispered, "that Pearl Lang came to Silver City at the same time you did. You haven't seen anything of her, have you?"

So the old vixen had finally worked around to it. This was the question she had wanted to ask all the time.

He considered the answer. For Pearl's sake he had better be cautious. "It might be," he said, "that she left the same night I did. I don't know about that, for she didn't leave with me. As to Silver City, I reckon she has as much right to come here as anywhere. It's mostly the business of her husband, isn't it?"

"Oh! Then you haven't seen her lately?"

"Not real lately," he said, hoping that such a small lie might be excusable.

"Well, it's been nice to meet you, Johnny Concho, and Mary sends her love, I'm sure. Is there anything you wish me to tell her?"

"Nothing special," he said. "Just tell her—tell her I'm working hard."

"Oh, yes, Johnny!"

He touched his hat and left. He wondered just what was the situation between Pearl and Duke. Would Duke come after her if he knew where she was, or would he be satisfied to see her away from Cripple Creek? Johnny didn't know about those things. Perhaps Pearl had told him right when she had said Duke didn't love her—or just what was it she had said? He couldn't remember.

He found the office. Ezra Smith was looking through his records, and Pearl, in her plaid dress and pert hat, patiently traced out mining claims on a large map of Black Mountain. Finally Smith lifted his face from where it almost touched the paper. "I reckon that's all I can do for you today, Miss Jones."

She considered the map. "This location on the north side of the mountain—Su Ah Ling—that's a Chinese, isn't it?"

"Yes, ma'am."

"He's probably not a citizen."

"I think he was born in California, Miss Jones. That makes him a citizen."

"A Chinese!" she said scornfully. "How much can I get that option for, Mr. Smith?"

"Maybe twenty-five dollars."

"I want it," she said suddenly.

"Very well, ma'am. I'll see if I can locate it tomorrow."

She turned as Johnny entered the office. "I've had a very good day," she said. "Would you believe it, I picked up a claim this morning for twenty dollars and sold it this afternoon for a hundred and twenty."

Johnny nodded. Somehow buying and selling did not appeal to him.

"Your sister is an intelligent businesswoman, Mr. Jones," said Smith. "You should be proud of her."

"I am," said Johnny.

They got outside. "We'd better have some supper," she said.

"All right—but stay away from that hotel where the stagecoaches come in. Mrs. Brown was waiting there when I went by."

Unexpectedly he saw Pearl's face whiten. "Mrs. Brown?"

"Yes."

"Did she—ask about me?"

"As soon as she could get around to it. But I told her nothing."

"Did she say anything—about Duke?"

"No."

She looked at him quickly. "Are you hiding something from me?"

He looked sidewise at her. "It strikes me," he said, "that you are more worried about Duke than you let on."

She shrugged, again in control of her feelings. "With a jealous husband anything can happen."

His eyes narrowed. "That's the first time you ever gave a hint that he might be jealous."

She started to answer, but hesitated. "I mean, speaking in general," she said. "Not about Duke particularly. Just in general."

"It had better be general," he said. "I've got enough troubles without a gun-totin' husband to look out for."

She put a hand on his arm. "You know what I told you, Johnny."

"I know," he said, "but sometimes I wonder if *you* do."

"Johnny," she said suddenly, "I have one more day to get the option that Eccles will pay eight thousand dollars for. You mustn't leave me now."

"What have I got to do with it?"

"Red had that option, Johnny, and he was supposed to mail it to you."

"He couldn't have," said Johnny. "He didn't know I was going to be in Silver City at all."

"If it was mailed it would find you, because everybody in Arizona knows Johnny Concho."

"But—tomorrow!"

"It *must* come tomorrow!" she said fiercely, and he was astonished at the burning light in her eyes.

"If Red mailed it before he died, then where is it now?" he asked.

"I don't know, Johnny." She was almost frenzied. "I don't know!"

"It could be held up in the mail somewhere—maybe."

"It has to be!" she said. "It *has* to be!"

Now he had something else to think about. Life was complicated enough, but he was beginning to wonder if life as a friend of Pearl Lang would be even more complicated.

They had supper and he went down to the stable to look at the horses. The liveryman came out. "That bay and that sorrel are yourn, aren't they?"

"Yes," Johnny said slowly.

"Sheriff was around here today lookin' at brands."

"Brands?" Johnny repeated.

"Yeah. The lady's sorrel is all right, but the bay you rode has got a Diamond Bar that the sheriff wants to talk to you about."

"He *wants?*" Johnny felt cold all over.

"He's inside now."

Johnny went in. The sheriff was a tall, thin man with the look of years in the saddle. "You own that bay?" he asked.

"Yes," said Johnny.

"Got a bill of sale?"

"Not—with me."

"In Arizona," the sheriff said, "a man always ought to have a bill of sale."

"I never thought about it," said Johnny.

"This here horse answers the description of a horse stolen by one Red Concho off the Diamond Bar ranch about seventy miles—"

"My brother never stole a horse in his life!" Johnny said belligerently.

"Your brother, eh?" The sheriff fished in his pocket for a piece of cut plug, and bit off a chew. "Yeah, makes sense. Tallman killed your brother and took the horse he was ridin', then pushed the horse off onto you when he run you out of Cripple Creek. What are you doin' in Silver City, Johnny Concho?"

"Trying to get a job."

"I don't reckon you find it easy, bein' Red's brother."

Johnny shrugged.

"Well, you better come along with me until we get this cleared up."

Johnny stared at him. "You mean I'm under arrest?"

"Since you put it that way."

For a moment Johnny thought of jumping him.

"Don't do it," said the sheriff. "If I can get this straightened out the way I think it is, you'll be free tomorrow. The telegraph wires are open till nine o'clock, and we won't get an answer tonight, but we should have one in the morning." He got up. "You come with me," he said.

Johnny followed him to the jail. The sheriff sat in his big chair and looked at a circular. "One bay horse, sixteen hands, nine-hundred pounds, Diamond Bar on left hip, believed stolen by Red Concho—"

"Don't say that!" warned Johnny.

The sheriff looked at him over the paper. "Hm. Got some pride, it seems. Well, come in here. Our beds are as good as any in town—and cheaper if you're innocent. Where you stayin'?"

"At the Withers Hotel."

"They won't miss you tonight." He opened a cell door. "Just make yourself at home in there. There's a couple of blankets." He went out and locked the door. "I'll do you a favor," he said, turning back. "I won't book you till tomorrow if you behave yourself. That way, if you're innocent, you won't have your name on the records. All right?"

Johnny snorted. What difference did it make what he wanted or what he agreed to? Everybody else did as they pleased anyway. If Johnny Concho got in the way, he got stepped on. Maybe Red Concho's faith in his guns had had a lot of reason.

He slept after a while.

About daylight the sheriff's wife brought him some ham and eggs, and Johnny ate wolfishly.

"You must be hungry, young man."

"I could've eaten a horse—raw."

She was a fat, happy-looking woman. "Young fellows like you, with a nice future ahead!" she said. "Why do you have to go around shootin' up the town?"

He decided not to disillusion her. "We just can't help it. Here is a town all achin' to be shot up, and here is a man rarin' to oblige. It's too much to resist."

"Well, it does give you a chance to sober up. More coffee?"

"Yes, please."

It was Pearl who got him out. The sheriff brought her in about seven o'clock and said, "Do you know this lady?"

Johnny got to his feet. "I figure I do, Sheriff."

"She told me the story the way I had it figured, and put up bond for the horse, so I reckon that turns you loose."

"Right kind of you, Sheriff," said Johnny. . . .

Outside, he said to Pearl, "Maybe I had you figured wrong. You been lookin' after me, all right."

"The way Red would have done?"

He looked at her. "Yes," he said, moistening his lips. "Maybe better."

They went up to his room, and Pearl sat on the bed while he washed up. He combed his hair and looked for his hat. It was on the bed behind Pearl. He reached for it, and she moved, and his hands were on her shoulders; then, without knowing how it happened, he found her in his arms, soft and yielding. He kissed her, and her lips were warm and moist, and she kissed back hard. Her arms were tight around his neck, and her weight almost pulled him over. But he saw the hat, and remembered what he had started to do, and jerked away from her and stood up, breathing hard.

"You don't act like a married woman," he said.

Her eyelids lowered. "Don't you think I have feelings, Johnny?"

He took a deep breath.

"I'll never see Duke again, Johnny."

"Maybe."

"I wasn't made to live alone."

He stared at her, fighting with himself. "You told me

once you were old enough to be my mother," he reminded her.

"You were worried then. I didn't want to worry you any more."

"And now you—"

"I like you, Johnny. You and I can go a long way together."

He shook his head. "This isn't right, Pearl."

She sighed. "All right, Johnny. It's like Red always said: you're too good to get anywhere by yourself." She got up slowly and straightened her dress. "If you change your mind, I'll be around. But don't wait too long. I'm a woman, you know."

"I know," he said harshly, and picked up his hat.

Chapter Eleven

THEY HAD BREAKFAST, and it didn't occur to him until they were almost through that he had already eaten once that day. About that time the sheriff came in.

"Sit down," said Johnny, "and have a cup of coffee."

The sheriff shook his head slowly. "I got bad news for you, Johnny Concho."

Johnny didn't move.

"Got a complaint sworn out by Amalgamated Copper. It says you deliberately and with malice aforethought destroyed fifteen mules to the value of forty-nine hundred dollars and three wagons to a total of twenty-four hundred dollars and copper carbonate ore of undetermined value. Anyway," he said heavily, "a total of seventy-three hundred dollars which I am supposed to recover. But since you don't seem to have much to levy on, they have also filed a criminal complaint of destruction of property, and I reckon, Johnny, I'll have to take you back with me."

Johnny stood up. "Pearl," he said resignedly, "there's no way to squeeze out of a levy that size."

Pearl looked defeated for the first time, but she said, "Johnny, I'll do everything I can."

"Don't waste the effort," he told her. "This time they will send me up."

"Who was the man who gave you the job with Amalgamated?" she asked.

"Blixen—but don't bother him. You might run across Eccles and spoil your deal." He saw the uncertainty in her eyes, and said fiercely, "Do what I tell you! This can wait!"

"Give me an order for your mail," she said.

He wrote on a slip, "To whom it may concern: I have authorized the bearer to get my mail in Silver City. Johnny Concho."

"Thanks, Johnny," she said, and stood up with him. He nodded.

The sheriff started off, and Johnny followed. He looked back once and saw Pearl headed for the post office.

He was locked in again and lay down on the cot to think it over. One thing was obvious: he was sure in the wrong place here in Silver City. The best thing he could do, if he got out of this scrape, was to go somewhere else as fast as possible.

He'd have to make up his mind about Pearl pretty soon too. You couldn't stay around a woman like Pearl forever without forgetting she was married. He knew the first answer: he ought to leave her. But how could you leave a woman who did everything under the sun to help you out?

And if he left, where would he go? West to California, south to Mexico, east to—where? Red had been at Rawhide for a while before he got killed; he must have been pretty well established there.

He finally went to sleep, and when he awoke it was dinnertime, and the sheriff's wife was there with a big chunk of pork roast, boiled potatoes, big slices of light-bread, and plenty of butter and coffee.

"I'm beginning to like this jail," said Johnny. "It has the best feed of any jail I've ever stayed at."

The sheriff's fat wife smiled shyly.

There was a hubbub in the outer office before he got through eating, and Blixen came in, shouting and waving a pair of gloves. "I told you," he said to the sheriff, "it wasn't Johnny's fault. And here's the proof!" He slapped the horsehide gloves on the table. "I hired him and he told me he could drive a six-mule team. He never claimed he could drive a jerkline."

"Yes, but he might not have said that to Williams."

"If something wasn't wrong, then how did McDonald get Johnny's gloves? I advanced Johnny the money to buy those gloves before he left, because his hands were soft, and I know damn well he wouldn't have left those gloves back there with McDonald if he could have helped it."

"What does that prove?"

"It proves McDonald and Williams were riding him. It proves he was tellin' the truth when he said he tried to get out of drivin' that jerkline. You know McDonald—and Williams has done his dirty work for years. What do you figure, Sheriff? They took his gloves away to punish him, didn't they? And if they did that, they prob'ly made him take the jerkline out too."

"It ain't too unreasonable," said the sheriff. "But I ain't no judge."

"That's what I figured. So I got you a court order, done up in black and white. This says for you to turn him loose!"

"All right," said the sheriff. "I do my best to go by the law. Sometimes it isn't easy, though."

Once again Johnny was on the street. "Blixen, I don't know why you did this for me."

Blixen chuckled. "I been feudin' with McDonald for thirty years, and this is the first time I really caught him with his handlebars down!"

"Lucky for me," said Johnny.

"Anyway, I like you, Johnny, and I figure you got plenty of trouble on your own as long as you're Red Concho's kid brother."

"What's that got to do with it?" Johnny demanded.

"Nothin', only Red didn't specialize in makin' friends. and they might take it out on you now that Red isn't around any more."

"It seems that way."

"You'll have to learn to take care of yourself some day, you know."

"So far," Johnny said thoughtfully, "I've found more friends than I figured on—but it can't last forever."

"Take my advice," said Blixen, "and leave the country."

"Leavin'," said Johnny, "I don't like."

"Didn't you like it when you left Cripple Creek?"

Johnny looked at him. "I guess you're right. I did leave Cripple Creek, and was glad to go." He looked at the distant mountains. "That seems like a long time ago. I'm seeing things a lot different now. I'm not so sure about leavin' any more, and maybe I'll change some more. I don't know. But I do know, like old Pete Henderson said, a man reaches a point where he gets tired of runnin', and I'm mighty close to that point now."

It was Saturday, and the town began to open up about midafternoon. The copper mines ran two full shifts, twenty-four hours a day, but Saturday was payday, and the hardrock men, the loaders, the hoist operators—those on the night shift, all toughened by four weeks of muscle-hardening work, long hours of swinging hammers and picks and shovels, long weeks without women, descended on Silver City to pry up the roof a little. If they didn't finish the job, there would be a new shift coming in about three A.M. to take over while those sober enough and still out of jail would go back to Black Mountain to dig for the red metal.

Johnny Concho observed these preparations and was well aware of the general trend of the evening. He ate supper with Pearl and thought about it—and about his future course.

Pearl said, "Johnny, why don't we go out for a look around, and maybe have a drink or two, shall we?"

He looked at her smooth bare arms, for she was wearing the wine-colored taffeta dress. "I don't think it's a good idea," he said.

"But, Johnny—"

"You're a married woman," he said, "and I'm tryin' hard not to forget that."

"But Johnny, Duke—"

"I know what you told me, but that don't change anything for me."

"Red wasn't afraid of Duke."

He felt a little sorry for her then. "Being afraid of Duke has nothing to do with it, Pearl. It's *you* I'm afraid of—if that helps any."

A strange look came over her eyes—a look he hadn't seen there before. It was as if she drew back from him in contempt, perhaps, although it was so quickly hidden that he had no time to be sure.

"All right, Johnny," she said. "That means you're going out alone tonight."

"That's what it means," he said, avoiding her eyes.

"I'll see you then, Johnny."

He got up, and she held out her hand, palm down. "You'll need a few dollars to celebrate with, Johnny."

He shook his head. "There's nothin' to celebrate." He swung on her suddenly. "Damn it, Pearl, do you think I'm doin' this because I want to?"

A new look came into her eyes—a look of waiting. "All

right, Johnny. What you say is always all right with me. But take this for drinking money."

"I can do without drinking."

"I know you can—but there's no reason why you should. If that option comes from Red, we'll both be rich. Take this ten for a good-luck piece."

He shook his head.

"Johnny—" She bit her lip, and he thought she was about to cry. "I don't want to think of you roaming the streets without even drinking money. Please take it, Johnny —for me."

He nodded wearily and slipped the coin into his pocket. Maybe a drink would do him good.

He stopped at the Black Mountain Saloon and had a couple. They warmed him up and eased his tension a little. He hadn't realized before that he had been as tight as a bobwire fence in a norther. He went on to the Hastings House to watch the stagecoach come in, and he was sitting there when Milo sawed his mules to a grandstand stop. Johnny hadn't meant to be seen, but Milo walked by him and unexpectedly turned. "Johnny Concho?"

Johnny stood up. "You name it," he said.

Milo seemed taken aback for a moment. "Nothin', Johnny, nothin'. Just been wonderin' how you was gettin' along."

"All right," said Johnny. "I'm doin' fine."

Milo paused. "That there Tallman—he's swingin' a heavy hand around Cripple Creek."

"So I heard."

"Got the whole town scared to death."

"Cripple Creek scares easy," Johnny said, trying to sound contemptuous.

"Uh—seen Pearl lately?"

"Who?"

"Pearl Lang—Duke's wife."

"Is she in Silver City?"

Milo looked at him, then walked on.

The passengers were claiming their luggage, and among them was a huge man with a shock of white hair, wearing a gunbelt.

Johnny stepped forward. "Help you, Reverend?"

Barney Clark whirled on one heel. "Johnny Concho! I heard you were here."

"Let me carry that grip."

"Kind of you," said Barney Clark.

"Just keeping busy," Johnny said.

"I thought you'd be taking in the town tonight."

"Later, maybe." He led the way into the hotel.

Three others were in line at the desk, and they waited. Johnny said, "You're preachin' at Rawhide, ain't you, Reverend?"

"I preach wherever the Lord calls me," said Clark, "and Rawhide is one of my responsibilities."

"You knew Red?"

"Ye-es, I knew your brother. Anything special you wanted to ask?"

Johnny saw the preacher's keen eyes on him, and it scared him from asking the question he wanted to ask. "I just wondered," he said.

"Rawhide is a different town with Red gone—and I hear Cripple Creek is some different too."

"You just come through there?"

"Yes. I saw Tallman standing by the door of the Copper Diggin's, watching the stagecoach. They say a peaceful passenger doesn't dare get off in Cripple Creek unless Tallman gives permission."

"It's your turn to sign up, Reverend. See you later," said Johnny. He set down the bag and walked out. Red, Tallman, Pearl, Mary—all mixed up.

He stopped and had a couple more drinks and began to feel good. His bruised face showed brown spots in the mirror behind the bar, but it wasn't very sore any more. The blisters on his hands were drying up. He was beginning to feel like a human being again.

He didn't see any six-shooters in evidence, and he guessed there was an ordinance that was being enforced, although the ranch hands were riding in from the country now and the hitching-rails were lined with horses, and occasionally a couple of shots were heard outside—all in harmless exuberance, most likely.

Then he became aware of an argument at his side. "I say Red Concho is not dead."

"The telegraph said he was."

The first speaker was a tall, thin man with a drooping black mustache. "The man never lived who could gun Red Concho in a fair fight."

"You don't know what a gunfighter is," the second man said scornfully.

The first man said, "Eat those words or I'll shove 'em down your throat."

The second man looked around wildly.

"Eat 'em!" the first man commanded.

"Just a minute there, mister." The lanky sheriff came out of the crowd. "Where you from?"

"Tucson."

"Well, mister, I don't know how they run things in Tucson now, but in Silver City we aim to keep order."

"You set against fun?"

"Not against fun—against people gettin' hurt—unnecessarily."

The man grumbled about a "town like this with no action a-tall," but the sheriff was already gone.

Johnny Concho had another drink and went out to the street. He started back for the hotel, feeling sleepy, but then he remembered Pearl waiting for him there and he decided against it. He stopped in at the place where he had first played poker in Silver City and had gotten in trouble because he had opened on less than two jacks.

A big game was going on at the same table as before. Mr. Eccles, his silk hat hanging on the wall and his bald head shining under the lamp that hung from the ceiling, his muttonchop whiskers flowing over the front of his shirt, had a big stack of gold coins in front of him. Blixen was in the game too, and his luck seemed to be running fair, to judge by his money on the table. Pearson and Benson were also in the game—both very conservatively, Johnny thought, and two other men—Rutledge from the Bar Seven Bar and Ezra Smith.

But most astonishing of all was Pearl Lang, dressed in the wine-red taffeta that was kind to her face. She was standing a little behind and to one side of Eccles, with a glass of whisky in one hand, and the other hand on Eccles's shoulder. Johnny stared for a moment. She seemed to feel the weight of his eyes, and looked up. Her eyelids were half closed, but she recognized Johnny and her mouth dropped open. Then she gave a quirk to one corner of her mouth, raised the glass and emptied it. She looked at Johnny and laughed and then suddenly hiccoughed. It caught her obviously unaware, and she lowered her face, while Johnny saw her turn red.

He moved around finally and got out of sight, but stayed where he could watch her. She didn't move away from Eccles, and Johnny nodded a little bitterly, even if she was Duke's wife. She wanted to sell that option, but she hadn't been able to get hold of it yet, and she was pouring a little female chloroform on Eccles's sense of duty to Amalgamated. No wonder she had insisted on Johnny's taking the money for a drink. She had had this in mind all the time.

He was appalled at her duplicity. After all she had done to make him believe about her feeling for him—here she was, acting like a dancehall girl from Santa Fe. Only she was playing for bigger stakes.

Eccles never looked up, never sensed the momentary change in her. He took a drink from the glass on the table and asked her: "What would you do, dear?" in a sort of pompous playfulness.

"Bet," she said without looking at his cards. "Raise."

Eccles looked up. His muttonchops moved up and down as he talked. "Gentlemen, I never ignore what a beautiful woman advises. I raise twenty-five on my possible pair of aces."

Ezra Smith said in his thready voice, "I have to stay."

Rutledge scowled, but called. Pearson shook his head and threw down his cards. Benson thought about it a long time and then called. Blixen called.

A gaunt, sandy-whiskered man stood behind Benson and craned his neck to peer at Benson's cards, which Benson was keeping fairly well covered with his hands.

"Competition," observed Eccles, "is the spice of business—just as variety is the spice of life." He reached up and patted Pearl's white hand. "Eh, dear?"

She finished her drink. "The race is to the swift," she said coolly.

Johnny took a deep breath. Maybe he didn't move fast enough for Pearl. Maybe it was a good thing. But it hurt his throat to swallow just then.

Blixen was dealing. "Cards?" he said.

Eccles took three, Ezra Smith two. Rutledge asked for five, and growled, "Easy way to go broke."

Benson had trouble deciding. He threw away four, then picked them up again, rearranged his hand, and threw away three. Finally he looked over his discard once more and selected one card from it, thus keeping three cards in his hand.

Blixen took three without looking.

Eccles said, "What do you advise, dear?"

Pearl, leaning against the back of his chair, said quickly: "Bet."

Eccles studied his hand. "I think you are overlooking a number of factors in the situation, my dear. However, I will place twenty-five dollars on the hand in the face of Mr. Smith's two-card draw and Mr. Benson's two-card draw. I am well aware that Mr. Smith does not bet twenty-five dollars on a bobtailed flush or straight, but I am not so familiar with Mr. Benson's principles of the game. Therefore a slight bet to flush the quail into the open."

Ezra Smith said, "I'll up it a hundred."

"You see, dear, he *had* three of a kind. The problem now becomes one as to whether or not he improved them."

Ezra Smith looked over his glasses. "Likewise," he said in his reedy voice, "whether you matched your two aces."

"I'm out," said Rutledge.

Benson said heavily, "I have to stay."

"My dear fellow," said Eccles, "no one is compelled to stay in. Likewise, no one is deceived by your apparent reluctance. No doubt you drew a pair to your threes."

Benson said nothing. Blixen called.

Johnny was now standing about six feet behind Pearl, but Eccles had his cards turned down. He rubbed his muttonchop whiskers, and Johnny realized that in that instant the game became a deadly one, for Eccles did not ask Pearl's advice; he was concentrating instead on the players and their draws.

All were calm but Benson, who drummed the table for an instant with his knuckles, and seemed about to break out in a sweat. Eccles noted this and picked up his own hand for a quick glance. Johnny saw them but made no

sign. The man had drawn three aces to a pair of queens
—an almost unbeatable hand.

The swinging doors banged open and a heavy-booted
crowd of miners surged in, led by McDonald and the
black-bearded Bob Williams. They were drunk and they
were noisy, and for an instant Eccles looked up in an-
noyance; then he concentrated again on the cards in his
hand.

Benson was getting red in the face—a man under high
tension. Was he getting ready to run a huge bluff?

Pearl said, "Bet, Mr. Eccles."

"You may call me Jonathan," he said, with his mind
on his cards.

He glanced again at Benson and said, not quite as carelessly this time, "Up a thousand, Mr. Benson."

Williams and McDonald led their gang to the bar and
ordered drinks.

Ezra Smith shook his head. "My threes will not justify
that kind of money."

Benson ran his hand inside of his batwing collar. He
looked at Eccles and frowned. Obviously this was a steep
game for him. Pearson looked almost as nervous, rubbing
his thumb back and forth across the point of his chin.
Benson swallowed and studied his hand again. He looked
over at Eccles and moistened his lips. "I'll raise you a
thousand," he said.

Blixen said, "I'm glad you gentlemen let me out easy,"
and tossed in his cards.

It was back to Eccles, and he wasted no time. "I'll
call," he said, and pushed out five stacks of double eagles.

Benson started to show his hand, but Williams hit a
man at the bar. Johnny caught a glimpse of Benson's
hand; the man had a jack-high straight flush in clubs.

But the other players had turned to watch the fight at
the bar. It surged toward the card table. The sheriff came
through the swinging doors, and a shot from somewhere
hit the lamp above the card table and spattered kerosene
over the table and the players. Then the other light was
knocked down and the saloon was in darkness.

The fight moved toward the table, judging by its
sound, and there was a creaking of wood and a crash as
the table went over, coins scattering over the floor. The

sheriff's voice came from back near the door: "Everybody stay inside! Nobody move!"

Heavy steps from behind the bar. An oath, scuffling. It stopped suddenly.

"Got 'em, Elmer?" asked the sheriff.

"I got 'em."

"Somebody strike a light—and keep away from that kerosene."

Half a dozen matches flared up. The bartender had two men by the collars. Eccles was sitting on the floor, still holding his cards. The table was on Benson's chest, but Benson's cards were scattered on the floor.

"How much money in the pot, Eccles?" asked the sheriff.

Eccles calculated. "Forty-six hundred dollars."

The sheriff whistled. "Stiff game."

"Wouldn't you—with these?" Eccles showed his full house.

"Reckon I would if I could afford it." He turned the two fighters over to a deputy and said, "Sober 'em up till morning." He looked around. "Who fired that shot?"

Nobody answered.

"Come clean," said the sheriff, "or I'll search every one of you."

A little man alongside Williams produced a single-shot pistol from the waistband of his pants. "I was just celebratin', Sheriff. First time I been in town for six months."

The sheriff looked at him as he took the gun. "Next time you tell me that had better be six months from now," he said.

The bartender lighted two candles on the bar.

Eccles held onto his cards.

Benson looked at them and said, "I've got you beat, Mr. Eccles."

Eccles hesitated. "Where are they?" he asked.

"I—they were knocked out of my hand when these gentlemen bumped into the table."

"That excuse won't win a poker hand," said Eccles.

"They must be on the floor," Benson said desperately.

Blixen had been picking up the money and counting it. "Eighty dollars short," he said. "That's not bad."

Eccles nodded, still sitting on the floor. Benson was on his knees. "The cards must be somewhere."

"None on the floor," said Blixen. "Maybe they went into the discard." He reached for it.

Eccles caught his hand. "No picking a hand out of the discard," he said firmly. "I don't want to be finicky about this, but there's almost five thousand dollars involved. If any disinterested person saw his hand—"

"He kept 'em covered," said the sandy-whiskered man who had been behind him. "I saw what he held but I never did see what he drew."

"I don't want to be unfair about this," said Eccles, "but I do not want to lose a bet without at least seeing the color of the cards." He looked around. "Didn't anybody see his cards?"

Johnny stepped forward. "I saw his hand," he said. "He showed it just as the fight started."

Eccles studied him. "Haven't I seen you before."

"You may have," said Johnny. "I've been around here for a while."

Eccles got up. "To protect myself," he said, "I will ask each of you to write down the cards Mr. Benson held. You," he said to the sandy-whiskered man, "write down the three cards you saw."

Benson, more nervous than before, hastily wrote on a slip of paper, folded it, and gave it to the sheriff.

The sandy-whiskered man, apparently not used to handling a pencil, wrote his three after some fumbling and considerable wetting of the end of a stub pencil.

Johnny took a slip and went over to the bar. He wrote, "Straight club flush. Jack high," folded it, and gave it to the sheriff.

The sheriff examined the three slips. "Well, Mr. Eccles. I reckon you lose," he said.

"On whose word?" demanded McDonald, the dispatcher.

The sheriff looked at him. "It was Mr. Eccles's proposition, and a mighty fair one."

McDonald pointed a long forefinger at Johnny. "On the word of a man who deliberately ran eighteen mules and a train of ore wagons off a cliff!"

"That's a lie!" shouted Johnny.

"Who you callin' a liar?"

"You," said Johnny.

"Wait a minute," said Blixen.

But McDonald and Williams closed in on Johnny from both sides. He went down under the battering hands of Williams, and, with his face smashed and pushed out of shape, he could not even shout when McDonald's hob-nailed boots scraped back and forth across his ribs like a Mexican border spur. The sheriff jumped in to push them back.

He heard Pearl scream and saw her throw herself at them. She was flung away by McDonald, and Johnny saw those hobnailed boots headed for his eyes. He squirmed and tried to turn, but Williams, astride him with his big legs, held him as in a vise. But a shot came from Pearl's direction, and McDonald shuddered as he was hit in the back. It must have been a small caliber, for the bullet didn't go through, but McDonald, trying to reach his back with one hand, slowly doubled over and fell across Johnny.

Williams picked him up, and now there was silence. The sheriff had Pearl's gun. "You better come with me, ma'am."

She went out, weeping hysterically.

Johnny got to his feet. Benson held out his hand. "Mr. Concho, I—"

"Johnny Concho!" shouted the sandy-whiskered man. "I got a good notion to take a poke at you myself."

Johnny looked at him coldly. "Why don't you? Every-body else has."

Johnny went slowly back to his room. He packed his carpetbag and went to the jail. "What are you aiming to do with her?" he asked.

"Something of a problem," said the sheriff. "McDonald will live—which some people think is a sad thing for Silver City, but the lady is liable for a charge of assault with intent to kill—and there are mighty few people in Silver City who won't bet you that McDonald will press charges."

"What's to be done?"

"Only thing I can suggest," said the sheriff, "is for her to take the first train out of town and keep going till she crosses the Colorado River. Arizona Territory is going to be unhealthy for this lady for quite a spell."

"Mind if I talk to her?"

"Go ahead. She shot him to save you. If I wasn't so old and so damn slow on my feet I'd have stopped this before it got started, but them two—Williams and Mc-Donald—they work like tornadoes."

Pearl was pleased to see him.

"You saved me from something bad," he said, "and I'd like to do something for you if I could."

"Go to California with me, Johnny?" she begged.

"Nope. I'm not runnin' any further. Any direction I take from now on will be back toward Cripple Creek."

"Does Mary mean that much to you, Johnny?"

"It's not just Mary. It's a lot of things."

"You sure you won't change your mind?"

"I'm sure."

"When are you going to pack your things?"

"I'm all packed. My bag is outside there."

"When are you leaving?"

"There's a freight train through about midnight, going east."

"You have no money."

"I'll talk my way."

"Johnny—" She breathed a deep sigh. "I might as well tell you something."

"I'm listenin'."

"Red isn't dead," she said.

He stared at her. "Red! Red isn't—"

"No, Johnny. Tallman was running a big bluff."

Johnny said in a low voice. "Pearl, if you're lying to me—"

"I wouldn't lie to you, Johnny. I know. You remember that day you rode out to meet the stagecoach?"

"Yes."

"And there wasn't any letter for you from Red? There was a letter from Red in the mailbag—for me. Red wrote it the night before, and he said he was leaving. He'd got in some trouble, and he was pulling out for a while, and he told me to stick close to you and I would find out where he was."

"And the day you got that letter, Tallman came to Cripple Creek and took over?" Johnny asked.

"Yes."

"Then Tallman didn't kill Red at all. He went to Raw-hide and found Red had lit out, so he came back to Crip-ple Creek and ran that bluff about killing Red. Well, I'll be damned!" he said with disgust at himself.

"That's it, Johnny."

"And that explains why you came with me, and why you stuck to me so tight, and why you kept after me to go to the post office."

"It was partly because I liked you, Johnny, I swear. And partly because I liked Red, and partly because I wanted to get those options from him. I bought the options in the name of Pearl Jones, and assigned them to him—"

"In what name?"

"His real name—William."

"Why didn't Red come up here to do his own dealing?"

"He was in trouble with the law. He killed a man up at the mines but I had already met him on the street in Silver City one day. I had won an option in a poker game and sold it the next day for twice what it cost. I told Red about it, and he had a big stake, and he said we'd go into business."

"What did he do with the money you made?"

"He put it back into options. He didn't need it himself. He put up the money and I bought and sold the options, and we split fifty-fifty."

"So," said Johnny, a new light coming over him, "Red isn't dead after all!"

"No, Johnny, just hiding out."

"But he didn't trust you. He was smart enough to make you send him the papers in between times."

"That's the way he wanted it."

"Then," said Johnny, "you've been dealing with Red's money since we got here?"

"Yes. I had been up here two days before and found out some options we would need, and I wrote him a letter at Rawhide. He was to send the papers to you at Cripple Creek."

"All right," said Johnny abruptly, "give me Red's half."

"Red's half of what?"

"His half of the money."

"What are you going to do with it?"

"I'm going back to Rawhide and set up in business."

"You can't do that, Johnny. The marshal—"

"I have violated no law in Rawhide. The marshal can't touch me for what Red did."

"But—"

"I'll buy me a horse and a pair of six-shooters," said Johnny, "and I'll ride into Rawhide like I owned the place. Do you think anybody would dare pull a gun on Red Concho's brother?" he asked with his jaw out.

"No, but—"

"Sure, some day there'll be somebody fool enough to call me—but by that time I'll be ready. I'm not a Concho for nothing. I can use a gun as well as Red can. I need a little practice, that's all." He took the coin pouch and divided the money, then took seventy dollars from his share and put it with hers. "That takes care of the money you spent on me and the money you advanced me. I'll buy a horse of my own, so you won't be stuck for the bond money on the bay."

She said softly, "I hope you don't get into trouble, Johnny."

"I don't aim to," he said, "but I found out something since Tallman hit Cripple Creek."

"What's that, Johnny?"

"The man with a gun holds the power—and I'm going to be the man with a gun!"

She looked concerned. "Johnny, you can't—"

He said fiercely, "I don't want to hear any talk from you. You followed me here and encouraged me to make love to you, just so you could get your hands on those options. You weren't looking out for anybody but yourself!"

"Johnny, that isn't fair."

"It's the way the cards fall," he said coldly. "And since I been looking out for myself without knowing it, I figure I can keep on looking out for myself."

"What about me?" she asked desperately.

"The sheriff suggested you better get out of town. I'll see Blixen. He's got no use for McDonald and Williams, and he'll give you a hand."

"Johnny, don't you like me?"

He nodded slowly. "But I don't trust you. You not only

followed me for the options, but you tried to finagle Eccles into giving you extra time. You want money. You want to live a high life. No wonder you left Cripple Creek."

"We could have gone a long way on that eight thousand."

"Sure—and later there'd be somebody else along with eighty thousand, and you'd be gone again." He studied her through half-closed eyes. "Take the train to Los Angeles. I hear there's plenty of action there, and I think you'll get along all right."

"Johnny!" She flung herself upon him, her soft arms around his neck. "You're sending me away!"

He loosened her arms and pushed her back firmly. "Sure," he said, "while I've still got my eyeteeth—because now I don't trust either me *or* you."

Chapter Twelve

JOHNNY CONCHO rode into Rawhide in the still of the morning, as Tallman and Walker had ridden into Cripple Creek. It was before sunrise, and a coyote ran down the main street ahead of him. His two walnut-handled six-shooters lay heavy on his thighs, and he knew he was in the right place. Even if word about his being run out of Cripple Creek trickled back here (as it might not do right away, for there was no direct connection between the two towns), it would be a long time before anybody in Rawhide would have the courage to call his bluff. In the meantime he would learn how to handle the guns. Then he would go on to Cripple Creek, and Tallman and Walker would have their game split down the middle.

Rawhide was a town something like Cripple Creek, but a little bigger, and he pulled up in front of the small Rawhide County Bank and tied the big sorrel horse he had bought in Holbrook. As he dismounted to wash his face in the horse trough, he thought momentarily of Pearl, but he didn't worry about her. He had stayed in Silver City long enough to be sure she got on the train—and now she was on her own. He had no doubt she could take care of herself.

He walked down the street, his gun handles slapping strangely against his legs. The guns were a lot heavier than he had ever realized. He turned in at the hotel. A kerosene lamp was burning on the desk, but the hotel clerk was nowhere to be seen. Johnny struck the bell several times and waited. Presently a small, freckled old man came out and said sleepily: "Somethin'?"

"A room," Johnny said. "A *good* room."

"Best we got, mister."

"How much?"

"Six bits a day."

"Fresh sheets every week?"

"If you're fussy."

"How about my horse?"

"Leave him at Blocker's Livery, back of the hotel."

"What's your name, old-timer?"

"I'm Bill Knox—Old Bill Knox, they call me. Was a fightin' fool in the days when this was New Mexico Territory, if I do say so myself. Want to put your name on the book?"

Johnny wrote in a bold hand: "Johnny Concho," and stood back to watch Old Bill read it. The effect was gratifying. Old Bill frowned, then read it again, using his finger to spell out each letter. Finally he looked up with his mouth open. "You're Johnny Concho?"

"Yep."

"Not—"

"Red Concho's brother," said Johnny.

Old Bill looked at his two six-shooters and swallowed.

"Well, Mr. Concho, we run a quiet place, and I hope you'll be the same."

"If nobody bothers me," Johnny said, "I don't aim to bother them."

"That's pleasant news, Mr. Concho."

"And by the way," said Johnny, hooking his thumbs in his belt, "if anybody asks, you can tell 'em Red will be back."

The old man stared at him. "Red's comin' back?"

"What I said."

"Well, do tell! You want to see your room, Mr. Concho?"

"Just tell me which one it is. I've got to take care of my horse."

"Head of the stairs, Mr. Concho. It's Red's old room."

Johnny nodded and went out. He untied the sorrel and rode it to the livery, where Ben Blocker was forking out hay.

"Got a regular stall for my horse?"

"Yeah, I think we can find somethin', mister. Nice horse."

"He'll need some oats and some clean straw. The name is Concho—Johnny Concho."

"The hell it is!"

"The hell it isn't!" Johnny said harshly. "Want to start an argument about it?"

"No, I don't argue with a Concho."

"See that you keep it that way, for Red will be back. He's just over the border."

Blocker nodded. "That's what I figured."

Johnny found a tiny eating place with a jackpine fire going strong in the stove, and said he'd have some fried potatoes, some beefsteak, a piece of pie and a cup of coffee. The girl who did the cooking was a small, yellow-haired girl built like a heifer on spring grass, and Johnny asked: "This your place?"

"Since my husband died," she said. "We had a little horse ranch, and my husband got tromped by a broom-tail."

"That's too bad. Any kids?"

"Three," she said, peeling a potato.

He studied her. "You don't look over eighteen."

"I'm nineteen," she said.

He looked around. "Where are the kids now?"

"In the back room."

"What's your name?"

She looked at him. "Expect to be here long, mister?"

"Maybe."

"If you're not, then you don't need to know. If you are, here's the rules: no huggin', no kissin', no nothin'."

He pushed his hat back on his head. "Doesn't leave much, does it?"

"Depends on where your mind is," she said sharply.

He bent his head to one side. "You're too pretty to be so unfriendly."

"I'm not unfriendly," she said, and leaned over the counter, "but I don't mind tellin' you I get tired of fightin' off drunk cowboys every Saturday and Sunday."

"You could maybe let up on the rules a little."

"When the right man comes along," she said, "the rules will be suspended."

"Some man is gonna be lucky."

She sighed. "No man in his right mind would marry a widow with three kids."

She dropped a big slice of steak in the skillet and it began to sizzle. "You can hang your guns on the wall, mister."

"They're comfortable right where they are."

"All right." She set down a cup of coffee and smiled. "But don't blame me if you spill gravy in the cylinder."

"I won't."

The door opened, and a man with a star entered. He sat down next to Johnny. "Concho?"

"Yeah," said Johnny, and the girl turned and stared at him as if for a moment she was turned to stone.

"Johnny, I take it."

"Yes."

"I'm Gompers, marshal of Rawhide. I don't want no trouble, Johnny Concho."

"Any reason I should give you any, Marshal?"

"Different people figure different reasons. However you figure, I want you to know I won't stand for any foolishness."

Johnny looked at him with amusement. "Strange you didn't tell Red about that."

"Red pushed me pretty far," said Gompers, "but I don't aim to be pushed that far again." He said, "Cup of coffee, Katie."

"Katie what?" asked Johnny, beginning to revel in his newly found power.

"Katie is more than *you* need to know," she said sharply.

"I call that right unfriendly," said Johnny.

The marshal looked at him. "I got a hunch, Johnny Concho, you're gettin' ready to take up where your brother left off."

"And?"

"We aren't going to like that, Johnny—Rawhide and me."

Johnny buttered a slab of bread. "Mighty friendly town. Don't see how my brother stood it—all this kindness."

The marshal finished his coffee. "You're a hell of a lot better-lookin' than Red," he said. "I hope you act better."

Johnny said, "Don't get any ideas, Marshal. I may be worse."

"That ain't in the cards."

The marshal left. Johnny finished his breakfast and paid for it. "I'm sorry, ma'am, that we got off to a wrong start."

She frowned—a very pretty frown. "It's better that way. Then we know where we stand at the beginning. I don't want a man thinkin' the wrong things and then have to slap his face. I try to keep away from the face-slappin' part."

"You're a good cook," Johnny said. "You ought to be married."

"Thanks. I'll put my mind to it."

The bank was open when he left Katie's, and he thought he would check on something. "My brother told me he left some papers here," he told the man behind the iron grillwork. "Do you know anything about it?"

"Your brother never left any papers here, Mr. Concho. In fact, your brother never dealt with us in any way. He may have left some papers at the courthouse."

"I just wanted to find out," said Johnny.

"Yes, sir, Mr. Concho."

He went into the saloon, got a bottle at the bar, and went to a table by himself. So far it was going all right. It was plain to see that the natives remembered Red, all right. That suited him fine. He wanted it that way. The feeling of power was coming back to him the way it had been in Cripple Creek, only this time it was stronger because he had created it himself.

A whiskered, bleary-eyed cowhand came into the saloon, looked around, and finally staggered over to Johnny's table.

"Yeah?" said Johnny without looking up.

"You Johnny Concho?"

Johnny poured himself a drink. "That's right."

"I'm Dan Mason. *Your* brother killed *my* brother."

Johnny, lifting the drink to his mouth, paused for an instant, then finished the motion and set down the glass. "Red killed your—brother?"

"Yeah. They had a fight over a slick-eared calf, and your brother gunned him down."

"Maybe your brother asked for it."

The man was swaying back and forth. "My brother was a peaceful, law-abidin' citizen. He never hurt nobody. Your brother took the calf away from him and my brother went after his rifle. Your brother shot him when he turned around."

Johnny considered. It didn't sound like a thing Red would do. Johnny poured another drink. "Sit down," he said without looking up.

"I'm not sittin' down with no murderer," said Mason.

Johnny kept his temper. "You're drunk. Better go home and sleep it off."

"I'm not drunk, s'help me. I'm sober as a judge." He pounded the table. "I swear it on a stack a bibles."

"Go away," said Johnny coldly. "You're rocking the table."

"I promised him I'd make somebody pay for that—and now Red's gone, but you come to take his place. I'll make you do the paying, Johnny Concho, through the nose."

Johnny sat back. "Will you get the hell out of here before I throw you out?" he asked.

A much bigger man came over. "Dan's drunk," he said, "but I ain't—and neither one of us is scared, if that's what you're thinkin', mister. Most of all, *I* ain't scared. You got them two guns just like your brother, but I'm sayin' to you now they don't scare me one bit, mister. And somethin' else: the man that starts somethin' with Dan finishes it with me."

Johnny's eyes began to narrow as he leaned back. He said nothing.

"You want trouble, mister, ask for Lem—Lem Johnson. I'm not much of a gunfighter, but I'll—"

Johnny jumped to his feet and glared at them. He was bent over, his fingers crooked as though he were about to dive for iron. "What's the matter with this town?" he shouted. "I never did anything."

"This town is just the way your brother made it," said Lem Johnson. "A right nice job he did, too."

Johnny rushed him. Lem was too big to move fast, and Johnny had him off his feet and rolled with him. Lem got both legs around Johnny's waist and held on while he hammered Johnny's face with weather-hardened fists.

He kept hitting Lem in the face, but Lem absorbed punishment like saguaro soaked up water. Johnny got free of the man's legs and jumped to his feet.

Dan Mason was coming at him from behind. Johnny sidestepped him and gave him a boot in the rear, and Mason went sprawling. Then Lem was back up and advancing.

"Stay back!" Johnny shouted. "Stay back or—"

But for some reason Lem didn't scare. He closed with

Johnny, and turned him, and then Mason, floundering to
his feet, took the whisky bottle by the neck and brought
it down with both hands on Johnny's head.

Johnny came to in jail. It was getting to be a familiar
kind of place. He felt the bump on his head, and it was
sore. His six-shooters were gone but his money was still
in his pocket. "Anybody home out there?" he called.
"Marshal! Marshal Gompers!"

The marshal came back. "How you feeling?"

"Beat up," said Johnny.

"Well, it wasn't exactly fair—two on one like that, but
Red didn't leave a lot of friends, as you may have figured
out by now."

"I'm not interested in that," said Johnny.

Gompers said, "There's no charge against you. You can
go if you ain't on the warpath."

"Against Johnson? I don't pay any attention to a man
like that."

The marshal looked at him curiously. "Well, that's different anyway. You had at least one chance to draw there,
but you didn't. That's different too."

"I could whip them both in a fair fight."

"Son," said Gompers, "I'm right glad to hear you say
that. Maybe them guns don't mean what everybody thinks
they mean."

"Don't make any mistake," Johnny said coldly. "When
the time comes, I'll use the guns."

Gompers nodded. He unlocked the door. "Man outside
to see you, Johnny."

"Me?"

"Yeah—man by name of Dark, Albert Dark."

"Dark!" Johnny followed the marshal to the office.

"Morning, Mr. Concho," said Albert Dark.

"Hello, Albert."

"Old Bill Knox told me you were in jail," Dark said in
his meek voice, "and I thought I might offer my services."
He was nervously turning his derby hat in his hands. "But
I see you have no need of them."

"You said there's no charge, Marshal?"

"Nope. Here's your guns—and I'd like to say something, Johnny. There's no ordinance against wearin' guns,

and I ain't sayin' I'll run you in if you do, but I'd sure appreciate it if you'd leave that hardware in your room."

Johnny stared at him. "And walk around town undressed?" he asked.

"You might save us both some trouble."

"What if I run into some more like Dan Mason and Lem Johnson?"

"You're apt to. That's what worries me."

"When I need your help, I'll holler."

"I want to warn you of one thing, Johnny Concho. After Red left, this town took stock of itself and we did some figurin'. We come to the conclusion Rawhide won't put up with any more one-man rule."

"That was *after* Red left," Johnny said sarcastically.

"Yes, after—but it goes just the same. We all got together and figured the only way Rawhide could get along as a town was to act like a town."

"What's that supposed to mean to me?"

"The people make the law, Johnny Concho. When the people are together, there's no gunslinger can take over a town."

"Guns kill," said Johnny.

"We know that—and maybe a man might get killed if a gunslinger started something, but the people are together. There'd be somebody else to step in to take his place. We aim to have law and order from now on."

Johnny glared at him, then turned to Albert. "Let's go back to that saloon and have a drink," he said.

"Yes, sir, Mr. Concho."

They went back and got settled at a table, and Johnny ordered a bottle of whisky.

The bartender hesitated. "You already owe me for a bottle—Mr. Concho."

"What bottle?" demanded Johnny.

"The one you took before. The one Mason busted over your head."

Johnny stared at him. He threw a half-eagle down contemptuously. "No wonder Red got the hell out of here," he said. "Give me the bottle."

"All right." He took a bottle from under the counter and pulled the cork.

"Give us glasses," Johnny ordered shortly.

He spun out two glasses. Johnny took them and the bottle and led the way to a table. He hooked his toe under a chair and pulled it out. "Sit down, Albert," he said.

"Thank you, Mr. Concho."

Johnny poured two drinks and pushed one over to Dark. "I suppose you're still trying to figure how to get back to Boston."

"Well, I would like to—but the truth is, Mr. Concho, I'm here on business." He swallowed the drink hastily. "Very important business."

"Anything I can help you with?"

Dark looked up. "I didn't hardly expect that—coming from you, Mr. Concho."

"Why not?" asked Johnny.

"If you'll pardon me, Mr. Concho, it's usually been the other way around."

"All right." Johnny scowled. "What's your trouble now?"

"Mary," said Dark. "Mary's gone."

Johnny stared at him. "What do you mean—Mary's gone?"

"Do you mind if I have another drink, Mr. Concho?"

Johnny poured it and watched him drink. Apprehension was building up in Johnny. "Now—tell me about Mary."

Dark put down his glass and shook his head slowly.

"She left Cripple Creek last week when she heard Mrs. Brown had seen you in Silver City."

Johnny said, "Then why are you in Rawhide, Albert Dark?"

"I knew she was going to find you, Mr. Concho, and I went to Silver City too, but the sheriff said you had come this way, so I figured—"

"You figured I would come back here to take up where Red left off. Is that it?"

"Well, yes, that's about—I hope you won't take offense, Mr. Concho."

"No," said Johnny. "All I care is: where is Mary now?"

Chapter Thirteen

THEY WENT BACK to the marshal and told him about Mary.

"I'll look out for her, Mr. Dark. How did she leave Cripple Creek?"

"She left home with a horse and buggy, but she sold them in Silver City and bought a saddle horse."

"Long ride for a girl—Silver City to Rawhide."

"She's quite determined," said Dark. "She's like her mother. I'm sure she could ride from here to Texas if she made up her mind to it."

"And Concho here?"

"She was looking for him."

Gompers nodded. "I'll let you know if she comes in, Mr. Dark."

"We better stop at the newspaper office," said Johnny. "They might of heard something."

"It sounds like a good idea," said Dark.

The newspaper was in a single room next to Katie's restaurant, identified by a piece of white cardboard in the window that said "Rawhide Citizen."

A man was sitting at a case throwing in type, and without looking around he asked: "Something?"

"We're looking for a girl," said Johnny. "Dark-haired, pretty, nice eyes—"

The man's arm moved, and four or five letters dropped into their cases with little clicks. "Any particular name?"

"Mary—Mary Dark."

"Where's she from?"

"Cripple Creek."

"You think she's headed this way?"

"She was," said Johnny.

"Have any money with her?"

"She must have had about three hundred dollars left after she got through buying the horse," said Dark.

"Three hundred dollars! Lot of holdup men in the hills, and plenty of them will kill for less than that." He put the rest of his handful of type in a galley and got down from the stool. "She could have come through

Holbrook or she could have come over the mountain."

"We don't think she came through Holbrook," said Dark.

The editor looked at Johnny's guns and then at his face. "Another one of them? I thought we was through with gunslingers in Rawhide."

"Meaning what?" asked Johnny harshly.

"Meaning it took me three years to get rid of Red Concho. Who are you?"

"I'm Johnny Concho."

"Johnny Concho!" The man's eyes blazed. "I'll tell you right out, mister, I'm not scared of your guns. Red tried to buffalo me for years but I never backed down an inch and I don't aim to start."

Johnny glared at him. "What can *you* do?"

"Write editorials. Tell the people how Red Concho is rustling cattle and stealing the ranchers blind—"

"Shut up!" roared Johnny. "My brother was no thief!"

The editor looked thoughtful. "If you mean he never was convicted—yes. But you'll have to go a long way, Johnny Concho, to find anybody in this part of the country who doesn't have his private opinion."

"They better keep 'em private," Johnny growled.

"Do you think you can help us?" asked Dark.

"Not much I can do, mister, unless I hear something. And that may not be for weeks."

"There must be something we can do."

"How long since she left Silver City?"

"About three days."

"Well, it's better than a three-day ride. I wouldn't worry, mister. Your daughter will turn up all right."

Johnny said, "Why don't you get a room at the hotel and get some sleep, Mr. Dark? I'll keep an eye open for Mary, and if she doesn't show up by morning we'll get horses and start looking for her."

"Mighty poor place for a girl to travel alone," the editor said, "unless she's acquainted with the country. There aren't too many water holes over the mountain."

Johnny led Dark away. To tell the truth, he had thought at first the older man was needlessly alarmed, but now he began to worry about it himself. There were not only holdup men but lions and renegade Indians in the mountain area. He got Dark a room at the hotel and went to the livery.

"Where would you go to look for a girl lost in the mountains on horseback?" he asked.

Blocker considered. "Well, I'd take this trail that leads off from the end of the street and bears south. You get out a few miles and hit a barb-wire fence. That's Sam Green's east pasture, and there'll be a gate if you follow it along. You cross that pasture with the windmills on your left, and you'll see a trail going up a pine ridge. Can't miss it."

"Saddle up my horse," said Johnny. "I'm riding out."

Blocker looked at him. "Mister, I run a livery stable. I saddle horses for women and old people—not for healthy young fellows like you."

Johnny was puzzled for a moment. In Cripple Creek he could order Joe Helgeson to saddle his horse, and Joe would do it even though he hated it. But here in Rawhide, where Red Concho himself had lived, everybody had their back up—and Johnny didn't know what to do about it.

"All right," he said. "I'll saddle him."

He rode the sorrel out of the corral and watched Blocker close the gate. Then he cut over to the street and found the trail.

He put the sorrel into a comfortable jog and as he rode he wondered about Joe Helgeson and his gold-ornamented saddle. That was one thing Johnny had wanted a lot. He didn't understand now why he hadn't taken it away from Joe when he could have.

He found the fence and went through the gate. He lined up the windmills and looked for a trail up the mountain. Then a man on a horse galloped across the pasture. "What do you mean, leavin' my gate down?"

"Well, I didn't—" Too late he remembered that he was wearing guns.

The man rode up; it was Sam Green. He looked at Johnny and his two pistols. "Christopher!" he said. "Who turned you loose?"

Johnny didn't answer.

"I don't give a damn how many pistols you carry. You get back there and close that gate or there'll be a shindig like you never saw before, Johnny Concho!"

Johnny went back, dismounted, and closed the gate. He remounted and started for the mountain.

"Maybe," said Sam Green, eying the pistols, "you better tell me what you're doin' in my pasture."

"Looking for Mary Dark."

"She supposed to be here in the hills?"

"That's what her father figured."

"Sharp figurer, that old cuss from Boston. Well, I tell you, Johnny—though I don't know any reason why I should —Mary Dark rode up to my place last night after dark, and my wife put her up. I reckon she's still there if you want to see her—and if she wants to see you."

"I'll ride up with you," said Johnny.

They rode to the ranch house—a big frame building, and around it a cluster of smaller buildings, some frame, some only roofs to protect harness and rigs, some corrals for breaking horses and for holding the night horses. This property was just across the county line from Rawhide, Sam said.

Johnny remembered to stay in the saddle until he was asked to get down.

Mrs. Green met them at the hitching-rail. She was a middle-aged, plain-looking woman with eyes that said a lot more than her face. "Company, Sam?" she asked.

"This here's Johnny Concho," Sam said.

"Concho!" Her eyes showed disdain. "First time I ever seen a Concho on our land in daytime!"

"Ma'am," said Johnny, tired of being insulted but not able to do much about it when the insulter was a woman, "Sam told me Mary Dark was here."

She shook her head, squinting her eyes and shading them against the sun. "Not no more, she isn't. I persuaded her to go back home, and she left a couple of hours ago."

"By herself?" asked Sam.

"She wouldn't let me send anybody with her."

"Which way did she go?" asked Johnny.

"Right up that ridge—only path there is."

Johnny threw the rein over the sorrel's neck. "I'll have to hurry," he said, and swung into the saddle.

"Nice-lookin' young man," he heard Mrs. Green say.

"—if you can forget who he is," said Sam impatiently.

Then Johnny was out of hearing. He followed the ridge at a fast walk, got down into a long slope among the pines and kicked the sorrel into a lope, slowed down again for some shale, then came onto another slope at right angles and pounded the sorrel's sides to gain time.

From the top of the mountain he caught sight of her far below, riding leisurely—too leisurely, for it would be dark a long time before she reached Cripple Creek.

He gained time until he got within shouting distance, and then began to call her name. He saw her stop the horse and look back; she turned his way and waited.

"Johnny!" she cried when he broke into the clearing.

He galloped alongside of her and stopped the sorrel in its tracks. He leaned over and took her in his arms and kissed her. She was warm and alive and she knew how to kiss back.

Presently they were walking on. She said, "How did you know where to look for me?"

He told her about her father, and she was distressed that she had caused him to worry, but, she said, "I am eighteen and I know what I want."

"And you want me. Is that it?"

"Well, Johnny, I still love you."

"Why did you come back from Green's place?"

"Mrs. Green said she was sure you weren't in Rawhide. She said nobody in Rawhide would ever again let a Concho get the upper hand there."

"She was talkin' pretty loud," he said.

"But don't you think it's right, Johnny? Do you think Red had any right to run Rawhide the way he did or Cripple Creek the way you did?"

"It's worse in Cripple Creek *now*, isn't it?"

"That doesn't make it right, Johnny. The only thing that's right is when the people are free."

"Nobody's in jail," he pointed out.

"My father has to pay Tallman one dollar out of every five he takes in. It's terrible, Johnny. Everybody will go broke in Cripple Creek if something isn't done about Tallman."

"I may get around to that," he said carelessly.

"What do you mean, Johnny?"

"These," he said, patting his six-shooters.

"Johnny, I've tried to tell you: shooting doesn't solve anything."

He held back the sorrel while she went ahead down a narrow path along the edge of a ravine. "It will solve Tallman."

"The way it solved you—so somebody else can come along."

"Then," he said, "what's the answer? Maybe there isn't any answer."

"There is one, but I don't know where it will come from."

"What does it sound like?"

"Somebody will run Tallman out of town without shooting, and after that there will never be another boss like Tallman, because the people will rise up as a town and will act together—and that's something you can't beat, Johnny: when people act together."

"Well, me," he said, "I've got my own plans."

"What, Johnny?"

He pulled alongside her. "I've got guns, and I can use them the same as Red did. I'm going to set myself up in Rawhide, and as soon as that is over I'll be up to Cripple Creek to take care of Tallman. You can tell him I said so."

"Oh, Johnny!"

"You're crying!" he said.

"Yes, Johnny, because you're so terribly wrong."

"How do you mean—wrong?"

"About guns and what they will do."

"They made a man out of me. I feel like somebody now."

"If it took guns to make a man of you, Johnny, what will happen when somebody takes the guns away?"

"Nobody *will.*"

"Johnny, if it really took that—if you're really like your brother Red—I don't think I'd love you any more."

"Is it so wrong to want to be a man?"

"Only wrong in the way you go about it."

"You have your way," he said presently, "and I have my way—but in the end somebody's got to pull a trigger."

"Even so, a man doesn't have to make a career out of killing."

"I haven't killed anybody," he protested.

"You've got to sooner or later, Johnny. That's what wearing those guns means. If you don't kill, you will get killed."

"I know one thing," he said. "If I'd had a gun at the copper mines, Williams wouldn't have beaten me up."

"Oh, Johnny, I'm sorry. But you were traveling in Red's shadow. It may take a long time to live it down."

His answer was stubborn. "I don't remember saying I was going to try."

They were silent for a long time. They came down a growth of quaking aspen with shimmering silvery leaves, and then they were out on the desert, and the sun, already below the western horizon, seemed to illuminate a great bank of blood-red clouds and send long red streamers out in all directions, while above the red was a great layer of vivid lilac. This eerie light shone for a few moments on the desert of cactus and sagebrush and sparse grass, and then it faded within seconds and left a deepening blue in the sky. Presently there were coyote barks, and a donkey brayed back in the hills at some Mexican farmer's adobe hut. Then the sky was blue-black all over and the night was filled with stars.

"I'll always remember you like this, Johnny," she said presently, "for I always think this is really the way you are—not the way you try to be when you buckle on those guns."

It was getting him—such talk. He said, "I'll see you into the edge of Cripple Creek, and then I'd better turn back."

"That's right." He felt her looking at him in the dark. "You might run into Tallman—and you're not ready, are you, Johnny?"

"No. No, I guess not."

She stopped her horse. "I don't want to see it when you come gunning for Tallman," she said. "And if that's the way you come, maybe I'll never see you again, Johnny." Her warm hand found his. "But if you throw the guns away and if ever you find out you need me, I'll be somewhere close, Johnny. Remember!"

"I'll remember." He took her in his arms and kissed her again, and it was the kind of kiss he could like the rest of his life, but presently he raised his head and touched her cheek with his hand and said, "I'm going, Mary."

"Remember what I said—if you need me, Johnny."

"Sure, I'll remember."

He listened to the hoofbeats of her horse grow fainter and fainter. Up ahead there was a light in the Copper Diggin's and another in Pete Henderson's office, and a glow in the window of Judge Tyler's place. Johnny fingered his pistols. Then he wheeled the sorrel and headed east. Sure, he'd remember—but by that time he wouldn't need her help. She would be needing him—and she'd be glad to have a man who could handle a six-shooter.

It was a long ride, and he didn't reach Rawhide until the middle of the next morning. He put up the sorrel and went to the hotel, and found Albert Dark pacing the wooden sidewalk with worry in every line of his face. He told him he had taken Mary home, and suggested they have a drink.

Dark almost cried from relief; he'd be happy to have a drink. He hadn't slept all night, worrying about Mary. And now he was very grateful, Mr. Concho, and he hoped that some day he would have a chance to return the favor. Naturally he wasn't any hand with a gun, and by this time his money was nearly all gone to Tallman and Walker, but he did hope he'd some day have a chance to repay the favor.

The editor saw them sitting there, and came over. "You found her all right?"

"Yes." Johnny told him about it.

"I'm glad," he said. "I'm real glad." He looked at Johnny. "You don't look like such a bad fellow," he said.

"I'm bad when I get started," said Johnny. "Don't let my looks fool you."

"I been fooled," said the editor, "but not in the last forty years."

"Have a drink," said Johnny, "and go back and write a great editorial about how you're going to chase Johnny Concho out of Rawhide."

The editor studied him. "Damned if you aren't *trying* to be bad," he said, and left.

The marshal was coming in the door. "Howdy, Si," he said to the editor.

"Howdy, Marshal."

The man with the star came over to Johnny and Dark.

"Know a man name of Duke—Duke Lang?"

"Yes," said Johnny, sitting up straight.

"Runs a saloon in Cripple Creek?"

"Yes."

"Had a wife named Pearl?"

"Yes!" said Johnny.

"Seems his wife run off to Silver City a few days ago, and he is right put out about it."

"Duke?"

"Yup."

"Pearl said they weren't—she said Duke didn't care what she did any more."

"Sonny," said the marshal, "let me tell you something When you get as old as I am, you won't never listen when a married woman starts talkin' like that." He shook his head solemnly. "It don't mean a thing, because all of a sudden the most besotted husband in the world will get his dander up higher'n a hawk watchin' a cottontail the minute he figures his wife has left him for somebody else. No, sir, you don't never want to believe anything like that."

"Pearl isn't in Rawhide. She was going west."

The marshal found a toothpick and went to work on his teeth. "Right now it seems he's not as much interested in gettin' her back as he is in shootin' up the man she run off with."

"Me?" asked Johnny.

"If you're the one she went away with—and I reckon you are, because you seem to know all about her."

"Is Duke here in Rawhide now?"

"He was at Katie's when I left."

"Has he got a gun?"

"Most decidedly."

"Can't you disarm him?"

"Johnny Concho," said the marshal, "I had your brother on my back for years in this town, and I sure as hell don't aim to make it easy for you to take over Rawhide the way he did. You'll fight your own battles, mister, and I'll pick up the pieces."

Chapter Fourteen

A.BERT DARK looked concerned after the marshal left. "I could buy a Colt," he said, "and help you out."

"No," said Johnny, "this is something I'll have to settle by myself."

"Did you—did you really run away with Pearl?"

"No, not really. I—"

"I've always wondered," Dark said wistfully, "what it would be like to run away with a woman like Pearl."

"There's one thing for sure," said Johnny. "She's full of surprises. I think, Mr. Dark, you'd better not pick a woman like Pearl to run off with. She's not the kind of woman you could handle."

Dark brightened. "Oh, I think I could handle—"

Johnny said, "Did you ever try to put a saddle on a snake?"

"Well, no," said Dark. "Not that I recall."

"I never did either," said Johnny grimly, "but I have an idea it would be about as easy as pinning Pearl down and knowing you'd find her there tomorrow. Pearl sorta makes up her life to suit whatever happens. She's got more tricks than an antelope with a busted leg."

"Well, Mr. Concho, what do we do now?"

Johnny had another drink. "You had better get out of range," he said. "Me—I practiced all night while I was riding on drawing these pistols. I got a hunch I'll give Duke his money's worth."

"You haven't slept all night," said Dark.

"I know that."

"Shouldn't you have some rest before you—"

"Let's go over and eat some breakfast. It isn't a very big town. Duke'll find me when he gets ready."

Dark's eyes were big as he watched Johnny put away twelve pancakes. "I've always read that the condemned man ate a hearty breakfast," he said.

Johnny asked sharply, "What do you mean by that?"

"Nothing, really, Mr. Concho. It just fascinates me the way you make those pancakes disappear."

133

Katie was leaning on the counter. "I was thinking about that myself," she said.

Johnny looked at her. "If you weren't such a good cook I'd ask you to marry me."

"That's not the way they usually say it."

"This is different," Johnny said, "because Rawhide needs a good cook, and the whole town would be roarin' mad at me if I took you away."

"You make me dream," she said, carelessly flicking a dish towel. "But anyway, Johnny Concho, I don't think you're much of a bet for a woman looking for a family man."

"Why?"

"Last night," she said, "you spent in the mountains taking one girl back to Cripple Creek. This morning a man from Cripple Creek is looking for you on account of his wife. I think you're in trouble, mister."

Johnny sipped his coffee slowly. "Katie," he said soberly, "trouble is my specialty. I been in more trouble in the last week than any ordinary person could get into in a lifetime."

"Well, I hope," she said, "that you two don't shoot each other up in my place. It's hard on the dishes."

"Madam," said Dark, "I will see that you are reimbursed for your dishes if Mr. Concho gets shot up in here."

Johnny said coldly, "That's twice you sold me down the river, Dark. One more like that and I'll say something you won't like."

"I'm sorry, Mr. Concho."

"All right. Now you sit out in front of the hotel. If Duke comes around, tell him I'm upstairs sleeping."

"And what will you be doing, Mr. Concho?"

"I'll be looking after my horse, for one thing. That was a long ride."

On the way he ran into Barney Clark. "You get around a lot, Reverend," he said.

"I have a number of small churches," said Clark. "They cannot individually support a pastor, but in traveling a wide circuit I can carry a little of the message to each community."

"You weren't preaching in Silver City, were you?"

"No, my boy. I went to Silver City to look into some mining options."

"Options? Do you know if my brother Red left any options behind him?"

"I knew nothing about your brother's business, I am afraid."

"Well, Reverend, will you be around for a couple of hours?"

"The Lord willing—"

"There may be a funeral to be preached this afternoon."

"I hope you're not intending to start trouble, my boy."

"I don't intend to start any, Reverend, but somebody else does. In either case, somebody will have to finish it."

"I am sorry to hear that."

"You got any idea about those options?"

"Ordinarily options are perishable property, being subject to a time limitation, but perhaps the county recorder would know something. I don't suggest this with anything in mind, for as I say I had little contact with your brother except indirectly—"

"How indirectly, Reverend?"

"Sometimes," said Barney Clark, "I had the sad duty of preaching the funerals of his victims."

Johnny, hearing this, hardened. He wanted no lectures about Red Concho. "I'll look into the recorder's office. Thanks, Reverend."

"You're quite welcome."

Johnny went down to the courthouse, a small square block of a building, and into a door with a sign hanging over it that said "Recorder of Deeds." He went to the counter and told what he wanted. The man listened without comment. Finally he said, "If there's anything here, I don't know about it—but maybe you better see the recorder. I'm just a deputy."

"Why didn't you tell me so in the first place?" Johnny demanded.

The man's eyes seemed to veil over. "You didn't ask me," he said.

The recorder was a younger man with a weathered face, and he looked more like a rancher than an office man.

"No, your brother never had any dealings with this

office, but you might inquire at the post office. He might have left something for you there."

He went back down the street to the post office, a tiny corner with a few mail boxes and a window; he had to pass through a drug store to find it at the back, sharing space with the pharmaceutical end of the business. Johnny looked in the window and asked, "You got anything left here by my brother, Red Concho?"

The postmistress was a woman—tall, angular, and also weathered from much time on the range. "Who are you?" she wanted to know.

"I'm Johnny Concho."

Her voice was a flat drawl, a little mannish but not unpleasant. "Red's brother, from all I hear."

"Yes."

She glanced at his gunbelt. "Taking up where he left off, seems as if."

Johnny drew a deep breath. "I came here to ask you a question," he reminded her.

"So you did." She picked up a small handful of letters from underneath a cast iron sleeping-dog paper weight. "It just happens that Red did mail a letter to you. I remember it because he said he was expectin' trouble— not that that was news to anybody in Rawhide, but it was sure news that Red was thinking about it. Well, he mailed this to you at Cripple Creek, but it was returned. Since it was mailed when it was, I reckon I'm within the law to turn it over to you now—providin' I'm sure you're Johnny Concho."

"I can prove it," said Johnny, watching the long, heavy envelope in her capable hands.

"You don't have to, I reckon. You're the spittin' image of Red, only you ain't redheaded and you haven't got the killer look in your eyes."

"Never mind that," Johnny said. "Give me the letter."

She slid it across the wood toward him. He noticed the wood because it was old and worn, and all the paint had been gone for many years, and the softer part of the wood had worn away, leaving narrow circular ridges of harder material that made the surface uneven, so that a corner of the heavy envelope caught on one and doubled up.

He took the letter and touched his hat.

"You're a lot politer than Red, too," she noted. "Never heard him thank a person in his life. He just took."

He opened the envelope and withdrew a sheaf of papers. He shuffled through them and saw the word "Option" on each one. A note on the bottom said: "Judge Tyler will know what to do with these." No salutation, no signature. Red seldom had time for things like that.

He carried the letter in his hand and went back to the hotel. "Seen Duke yet?" he asked Albert Dark.

"He was in the bank a while ago, Mr. Concho."

Johnny gave him the letter with the papers inside. "If anything happens to me, turn these over to Mary and tell her to take them to Judge Tyler. No, wait a minute." He remembered Tallman and his twenty per cent. "Tell her to take these to Silver City and see a broker named Ezra Smith. He'll tell her what to do with them. There's one in here that may be valuable."

"Yes, sir, Mr. Concho."

"Now," said Johnny, "I'm going up to get some sleep. I'll need a steady hand when I meet Duke."

Albert Dark swallowed hastily. "Yes, sir. Shall I tell him—"

"Tell him to hang around, or, if he can't wait, tell him to pound on my door."

He went upstairs, pulled off his boots, hung his gunbelt over the brass bed-post, and lay down. It was one of the finest feelings he had ever had, and his eyes closed almost immediately. He could feel himself going to sleep. . . .

He awoke to a hammering on the door. His eyes opened wide, and he leaped for his gunbelt. Then Albert's voice came: "Duke is threatenin' to come after you if you don't come down, Mr. Concho."

Johnny was wide awake. He said, "Tell him I'll be right down."

He buckled on his gunbelt and went to the window. Duke Lang was standing across the street by the harnessmaker's, a gunbelt on his hips and a single gun on his right side.

Johnny turned back and took his hat from the other bed-post. He pulled it onto his head. He put on his boots and went to the door and opened it. He wasn't nervous now—the sign, he had heard, of a real gunfighter. No, he wasn't nervous at all. A little tense, but not nervous. He went down the stairway. "I owe you for my room," he told old Bill Knox.

"You're leaving, Mr. Concho?"

"I don't know," said Johnny. "I'm just paying up my bills as I go."

"Not everybody is that thoughtful," said Bill Knox.

Johnny said on impulse, "Give me a receipt."

"Yes, sir."

The tightness within him was growing, but he could think of no other way to delay the meeting. He glanced around the room. Albert Dark, in his derby, was sitting near the door like a sentinel.

"Albert, let's go get a drink."

"Yes, sir, Mr. Concho."

Johnny went out first. He saw Duke stiffen, but he turned to the left.

Duke's voice rolled across the street: "Johnny Concho!"

Johnny didn't turn. "Be back in a minute," he said.

He led the way into the saloon. Dan Mason and Lem Johnson were standing at the bar. Mason saw Johnny and nervously threw his drink into his mouth, spilling some of it. Then they both walked out.

Johnny leaned on the bar. "Give us a good one," he said.

The bartender reached to the back bar.

"Not that Taos lightning," said Johnny. "Give us some of that there Lexington Club House."

"That's twenty cents a drink."

"Twenty cents?" Johnny raised his eyes. "The price of dying is going up. Well, set it out here!" he said.

"Yes, sir."

Johnny had two drinks—no more. Then he hitched up his belt, hooked his thumbs in it, and said, "Come on, Albert. Let's see what the man has to say."

They went out of the door. "Stay behind me," said Johnny. "To one side—and don't interfere."

"Yes, sir, Mr. Concho."

He heard Dark's voice fade as he strode into the street.

This was noon, and the sun lay heavy on the hot dust of the street. It was warm on the backs of his hands, for the sun was almost overhead.

Duke Lang saw him at once, and angled across the street to meet him. Duke's call came clear in the midday quiet: "I'm going to teach you a lesson, Johnny Concho."

Johnny kept moving. He was glad his feet didn't falter. "Be sure you're big enough," he said.

"I'm big enough," Duke growled. "I saw you that night in Cripple Creek. Remember you and Tallman?" Duke's bitterness grew suddenly violent. "I saw him make you run with your tail between your legs like a whipped coyote."

Johnny knew then what was Duke's greatest strength: that he had seen Johnny run. Johnny's mouth tightened. This would be no repetition of the night in Cripple Creek. He might die, but he wouldn't run.

They were thirty feet apart, and Duke was still coming on, his arms hanging at his sides. "Two guns," Duke said scornfully. "But it's the man behind the guns that counts. You're not the man, Johnny. You can't beat me to the draw."

Johnny kept his feet moving. He and Duke were twenty feet apart. Johnny felt the heavy six-shooters slapping his thighs. His hat was pulled down low over his eyes, but he was watching Duke. He saw Duke's hand move toward his gun, and Johnny's hands both moved back; his fingers curved and he got ready to drop them.

Fifteen feet apart. Duke dived for his gun and brought it up. But Johnny stood there, his fingers still curved, his hands still hovered above his guns. In that fraction of a second that separated him from eternity, Johnny saw uncertainty go over Duke's face, then hardness. "You won't draw, eh?" Duke didn't fire.

Johnny didn't know what held him back. It must have been fear, but he didn't feel scared. He'd heard that fear paralyzed a man, but he wasn't paralyzed.

His hands dropped slowly; his fingers uncurled; his arms straightened until his hands were at his sides. Duke took up the measured walk again, his face now suffused by hate. "You won't draw, Johnny Concho! You're a coward, and you're trying to cheat me out of my revenge. But you'll pay anyway, Johnny Concho. I won't kill you, but you'll wish I had!"

As Johnny stood there with his arms down, Duke Lang

stopped no more than two feet away. He reversed his pistol as he raised his arm, and brought the muzzle down on Johnny's head. It stunned Johnny and knocked his hat off. He shook his head, but Duke slashed him again, and this time the front sight tore open a great patch of scalp. Duke hit him again, and dragged the front sight down to his forehead. Then, with Johnny's knees buckling from the blows on his skull, Duke went wild. He slashed Johnny's skull; he raked that murderous front sight across Johnny's face from one side to the other and back again, until Johnny could no longer see because of the blood in his eyes.

Vaguely he knew that somebody caught Duke's arm, and he saw people crowding around. He saw Katie's bright golden hair in the sunshine, and he sank down into the thick dust of the street, no longer in pain but very, very tired.

He came to on his back. His eyes were clear but he could see nothing but a lamp on the wall. Then he heard a soothing voice: "All right, Johnny Concho. Feel like sitting up?"

Johnny's arms were all right. He pushed up and saw Albert Dark standing behind the doctor.

"Here. Try a drink of whisky," said the doctor.

Johnny's lower lip was split and it stung sharply when it touched the glass, but he swallowed a little. His head felt sore all over, and inside it pounded like shod hoofs on cobblestones. He shook his head, and it was ten times worse, so that he tightened his stomach and arched his neck for a moment. Finally he opened his eyes. "Let me have another," he said.

"Sure. Take it easy. Nothing wrong that a few days won't heal."

"Nothing?" asked Johnny. "You mean nothing on the outside."

"Duke is gone, Mr. Concho," said Albert Dark.

Johnny thought about it. "I didn't have it coming," he said, "but I guess I don't blame him. I saw her in Silver City, and I think I know how he felt, because she must have done that many times while they were married."

"Why did Duke pick you?" asked the doctor.

Johnny tried to smile, but it hurt too much. "It didn't make much difference. He had to take it out on somebody to save his own hurt and his own pride, and he figured I was the easiest one to take it out on."

"If you're all right," said Albert Dark, "I'll have to be getting back home. Sarah will be wondering what happened to me."

"Sure. Thanks, Albert, for siding me."

"It's all right, Mr. Concho. It was a pleasure. I mean— I wish you had shot it out with him, but—" He faltered.

"I know what you're thinking, Albert." Johnny's voice was a little bitter. "It would have been better if I had at least drawn a gun to protect myself—but it was a funny thing, Albert. I never thought of it!"

Albert's face was twisted up as he tried to understand.

"Out there in the street," Johnny said, "I kept waiting for *him* to make the first move—and the second— and the third. By that time I didn't know what was happening."

"It's the first move that counts," said the doctor, nodding.

Johnny thought about it. Finally he looked at Albert Dark. "I want you to take my guns and the gunbelt," he said. "They're no good to me." His jaws hardened at the corners. "I haven't got the courage to draw a gun!" he said.

After Albert left, Johnny paid the doctor and went to his own room. His head and face were bandaged until he was unrecognizable, but he could still think, and the thoughts went down bitter trails:

As Red Concho's kid brother in Cripple Creek he hadn't known what he was doing; he'd been a kid playing at a man's game;

As Red Concho's kid brother in Silver City, he had been helpless without guns;

As Johnny Concho in Rawhide he had been helpless *with* guns.

In any case he had a long way to go to get out from under the shadow of Red and the people's hatred of Red. Somehow he would have to be himself—without guns— and he faced it: he would not find it easy.

He wept in fury at his own littleness—not sobbing cries,

but a few tears whose salt bit into his raw flesh and made him face the next move. Where could he go? He got up from the bed, weary and beaten, aware now of his own weaknesses and his own shortcomings. He would have to leave. There was no place in Rawhide for him; they would hound him as they had in Cripple Creek and Silver City. He would have to leave . . . go away to some place where they wouldn't know anything about Johnny Concho. . . .

The people of Rawhide watched him go silently, peering from windows and doors. He knew they were glad to see him go. He went to the stable and harnessed the sorrel. He paid Blocker his bill and turned the horse to ride out to the south to keep from going down the main street, and there was Barney Clark, his shock of white hair like a halo around his head. Clark walked up and put a hand on the sorrel's neck.

"Where to now, Johnny?"

Johnny waved vaguely. "Somewhere. Anywhere."

"No guns?"

"I'm not man enough to use them," said Johnny. He rose in the saddle. "But I'll tell you something, Reverend. Some day I'll come back—some day when my brother Red returns from wherever he is. We'll come here and make this town eat crow!" It was a last gesture of defiance to a world that was against him.

Barney Clark just looked at him. "You think Red will come back from where he is?"

"I know he will," said Johnny. "He's my brother!"

"It will be a good trick," said Barney Clark, "for your brother is in hell if my judgment is any good."

Johnny stared at him, suddenly feeling weak all over. "You mean Red is dead?"

"Dead as a doornail. Tallman killed him one afternoon about a week ago. I preached his funeral sermon and saw him shoveled in. I can show you his grave."

"If that is so," Johnny said, "why didn't somebody around here tell me?"

"Maybe," said Clark, "you never asked them."

Chapter Fifteen

JOHNNY HEADED SOUTH, up the valley. For the first day he punished the sorrel in his fury at himself. He camped out that night where the sorrel could graze, and the next morning he stopped to eat and bought some oats for the horse at a small mountain town.

He crossed the stream that second day, pushing the sorrel without letup. The stream was still full—knee-deep from the runoff of snow in the mountains.

To the west now was a long slope of gray-brown rocks lightened by the bright green leaves and coral blossoms of loco weed, and higher were the silver of quaking asp, the yellow green of birch, and the deep green of pine or cedar, with occasionally a tall, dead, white-barked tree trunk standing over them all with leafless branches like a scarecrow's arms. Up this valley he went, the pace a little slower. He stopped at a spring and soaked his bandages and painfully removed them, but the bleeding started and he knew he needed new dressings.

He stopped at the next town, down in the valley—a town a lot like Cripple Creek—and looked for a doctor's office. He saw a marshal standing in a doorway watching him, and stopped the sorrel.

The marshal stepped down. "Been in a fight, mister?"

"Yeah. Know where I can find a doctor?"

The marshal studied him. "Ain't you somebody I ought to know?"

"I don't know who you're supposed to know," said Johnny.

"Ain't you Johnny Concho?"

"What if I am?"

"Brings up some other facts," said the marshal, squinting up at him. "Got a nice, quiet little town here, and I aim to keep it that way."

"I was looking for a doctor," Johnny said stiffly, "and no lecture."

The marshal walked closer. "You been pistol-whipped, ain't you?"

"No," Johnny said coldly. "I woke up in bed with a buzz saw."

"I'll send you to a doctor, Johnny Concho. You're bleeding and you need some bandages—but I want to tell you one thing."

Johnny waited, feeling the breath build up inside of him.

"As soon as he gets you fixed up, move on out of town!"

Johnny asked, "Do you see any iron on me?"

"No, but you're a Concho—"

Johnny glared at the marshal. Then he spurred the sorrel down the main street in a cloud of dust.

Later he was sorry, for the sun baked his wounds, and the flies buzzed around his head, and his scalp was so cut he couldn't put his hat on, and the wounds bled periodically, adding to his discomfort, and his head and face ached unbearably.

He rode into another town just before dark, and spotted a doctor's shingle. He stopped the sorrel outside and dropped the reins on the ground.

The doctor frowned when he saw him, and shook his head. "You should have had attention before this, mister."

"Go to work," said Johnny.

"It's going to hurt."

"Got any whisky?"

"Yes, I have."

"Pour me a pint."

He drank it out of the bottle until it was half empty, and after a few minutes he began to feel numb. "Start," he said.

"I'll have to clean you up with alcohol. The wounds are probably very dirty."

"Hell of a waste of alcohol," said Johnny.

"It will burn pretty bad."

Johnny spoke tightly. "I said go ahead!"

The doctor nodded. He soaked a piece of cotton with alcohol and began to wipe. At first the rubbing action against the raw wounds added intolerably to the ache, but then the alcohol began to bite, and the burning was so intense and so deep that Johnny forgot about the ache.

The doctor cleaned up the wounds and put vaseline on

them and rebandaged his face and head. "It looks almost like you had a pistol-whipping, mister," he said at last.

"You're a damn smart doctor," Johnny said. "How much do I owe you?"

"Two dollars for the call, fifty cents for the bandages, seventy-five cents for the whisky."

Johnny paid him, and the doctor shook his head again as he looked Johnny over. "You're a regular mummy," he said. "Your own mother wouldn't know you."

"I never had a mother," said Johnny, now drunk. "I was weaned by a Gila monster."

Running, running. No place to stop. No place to rest. He camped out at night. By day he ate in restaurants while the townspeople stood in awe of his bloody bandages. He hit open desert and turned east and finally followed a river bank north because there was nowhere else to go. The sorrel's ribs were showing, but Johnny never stopped pressing.

One evening before sundown he was sitting at a fire, baking two potatoes that he had bought in the last town. He was watching his backtrail, and he made out a rider coming slowly toward him. He got behind a boulder and waited until the rider came into the clearing. Then he stood up straight, with the sun in his eyes, and shouted: "What do you want?"

The rider turned his way, and he heard Mary's scream. Her horse reared and she fell out of the saddle, and he ran to catch the horse's reins. She finally got on her feet, her face white. "Johnny!" she cried.

He held her with both arms and tried to soothe her, but she was almost hysterical. "Johnny, what did they do to you?" she kept saying over and over.

"Not too much." He smoothed her hair gently with his fingers. "I can forget it—now that you are here."

"I'm sorry, Johnny."

"I didn't mean to frighten you," he said. "Where you going?"

"I've been looking for you, Johnny."

He frowned the best he could under the bandages. "I been moving pretty fast. How did you find me?"

"You went through a lot of towns."

He hardened. "And every town had the same story:

'Sure, he was here, but the sheriff ran him out. We've got no room for Johnny Concho in our town.' "

Mary said, looking at him, "That's about the way it went."

"Johnny Concho," he said bitterly, "tough guy." He pointed to the fire. "You're just in time for dinner. Got a couple of potatoes wrapped in clay, down in the ashes. They'll be good in another half an hour."

"Johnny, is that all you've got to eat?"

He shrugged.

"But—two potatoes!"

"It scares people when I go into a store," he told her.

Presently she asked, "Johnny, what are you going to do?"

"I been figurin' that out the last few days," he said, "once my head quit hurting so much. I've got my mind set on California. Nobody knows me out there."

"They say that Pearl had gone to California."

He stared at her. "Then maybe I'll go to Texas—or Montana."

"Johnny," she said, "what about you and Pearl? Is it all over with, or is that why you mentioned California?"

He snorted. "There was never anything to start with. Pearl followed me of her own free will. I might have liked Pearl, all right—but she wouldn't let me. Pearl is too busy looking out for herself."

"So there wasn't anything between you?"

"Never was. Pearl used me to get away from Duke."

"The—"

"Don't say it!" He shook his head. "Pearl has got plenty of faults—more faults than anything else—but she was generous and she stood by me—even if it was lookin' out for herself."

"Johnny, do you have any money?"

He poked the fire with a stick. "Plenty."

"With two potatoes for supper, I guess probably you have. . . . How much, Johnny?"

He grinned. "Two dollars."

Mary said, "I want to go with you, Johnny, wherever you go."

He stared at her. "You're out of your mind."

"Do you think I came this far to say good-by?"

"You didn't come scouting for Tallman, did you?" he asked suddenly.

She looked at him reproachfully.

"I'm sorry, Mary. I've gotten so I don't think straight."

"Aren't things getting cleared up a little?"

"Two or three times lately I thought I had the answer —but every time I thought so, I found out the answer was different." He got up and walked away, then turned. "So you love me," he said. "You don't even *know* me!"

"I know enough, Johnny. There's enough for me to love."

"How can you say that when I don't know myself?"

"You're like a small boy, Johnny, only you're having to grow up fast—terribly fast. You always had Red to look out for you, but all of a sudden you were on your own, and you didn't know where to turn or what to do. You mustn't give up, Johnny. It takes time to work these things out."

But suddenly Johnny felt very low. "You don't want any part of Johnny Concho," he said. He turned suddenly and shouted at her: "Go home! Get away from me! Get away before the maggots start hatching in this dead carcass!"

She just shook her head. "Johnny, Johnny!" she said softly.

"I've got nothing to offer you. I'm a dead-beat, a no-good. I can't even stick up for myself when I've got two guns in my holsters."

Mary said quietly, "It's not because you were afraid, Johnny. It's because you couldn't kill—you're not a murderer." She went on, "There's only one thing I've always wanted, Johnny—to be with you."

He turned to look at her. "You don't know what you're letting yourself in for. What am I going to do with the Concho name—change it? Or move to some place where it isn't known? And how am I goin' to take care of you? No food, no money to buy it. My horse eats grass all night because I can't buy oats. And you want me to look after you!"

She got up. "It's worth a lot," she said, "to know that you are thinking about that." She went to where her saddle was lying under a tree. She opened one of the saddlebags and took a small package out of it. She walked back to the fire and offered it to him. He shook his head. She sat down, took off the string, and revealed a handful of paper money.

"Three hundred dollars," she said. "Enough to take us both a long way."

He looked at her, then turned and walked away. But she followed. "It's what I want, Johnny."

He turned to face her. "Are you sure?"

"I'm sure."

Johnny drew a deep breath. "All right. I guess you've got a partner."

Mary asked, "A partner?"

He looked at her quickly, and it dawned on him what she meant. "A husband," he said slowly.

"It's a deal, then, Johnny?"

"It's a deal," he said.

"Oh, Johnny!" She threw her arms around him and buried her head in his shoulder.

"Hey," he said, "your tears are goin' through my shirt!"

She started to draw back, but he held her and kissed her hard.

The next morning they started up without breakfast. It was a beautiful morning in the hills, and the sun was warm and welcome after the cool night, and they were not in a hurry, but presently they came to a town, and Johnny said, "You go in and buy some grub. I'll meet you on the other side."

"Afraid, Johnny?"

"Not exactly—but there's no use askin' for trouble."

"All right. I'll meet you on the other side."

She met him with coffee and potatoes and meat, and they rode on to a small spring hidden among the trees, and took their time about eating. The sun began to warm up, and they moved on. Early in the afternoon they approached another town, and stopped to study it.

Johnny asked, "What do you think?"

"We have enough grub for today," she said, "Maybe we should move on."

"You want to get married, you said."

"Yes—if you do."

"Then here's where we do it," said Johnny.

"What if there's trouble?"

Johnny grinned. "So far it's had no trouble finding me." He led off. "Let's go."

At the door of a saloon he saw Josh, the swamper at the Copper Diggin's. Josh stared at him until they were directly opposite. Johnny kept Mary hidden behind him.

"Howdy!" said Josh.

"Who does the marryin' in this town?" asked Johnny.

"That'd be Barney Clark, up there at the church. He's there today, too."

"Up there at the church?" Johnny squinted.

"Up on top of the hill. It's a little place, but it's nice."

"How long you been here?" asked Johnny.

" 'Bout a week." Josh got up lazily. "Have I seen you before, mister?"

"You might have," said Johnny. "I cover quite a bit of country."

Two men came to the door behind Josh. "Who is it, Josh?"

"I ain't sayin'."

Dan Mason pushed Josh aside and stood in the doorway. "A right pretty sight, I must say. Nice-lookin' gal, too. Howdy, ma'am."

"Hello," said Mary, while Johnny watched Mason closely.

"You didn't say who they was?" Mason said to Josh.

"Ask for yourself, mister," said Johnny.

Mason looked at him. "I got a hunch—but I'll find out my own way."

Johnny felt himself tightening up. He said to Mary, "Let's find the preacher."

"A wedding party, eh?" said Mason. "Ain't that nice!"

Lem Johnson called out from the doorway: "Could that be Red Concho? Lot of stories goin' around about Red. Some say he's dead; some say he isn't."

"Hard tellin'," said Mason. "He ain't wearin' no hardware."

"Maybe that's a part of his disguise."

Johnny rode off slowly, making sure that Mary followed.

"One thing I never heard of," said Lem Johnson behind him. "Red Concho gittin' hitched!"

Chapter Sixteen

THE CHURCH was a small building, and by the looks of
it had once been a store or a mine office. Next to it was a
two-room frame house, and they rode up to the front.
"Hello!" called Johnny. "Anybody home?"

A small gray-haired woman opened the door. "If
you're lookin' for the reverend, he'll be in from the pasture in a little while." She shaded her eyes against the
sun and stared at Johnny. "Or are you lookin' for the doctor?"

"We want a preacher," said Johnny.

"Well," she said, "they do get married in some out-
landish outfits these days."

"How long is it," asked Johnny, "before the reverend
will be back?"

"Not very long now. Why don't you two go into the
church and wait? It's cooler in there."

"All right."

"One thing," she said. "Have you got a license?"

"No," Johnny said. "Hadn't thought of it."

She chuckled. "Mostly they don't. Well, you'll need a
license—which you can get down there at the clerk's office. He ain't a county clerk, but the county is so big they
put a deputy over here for such things."

"I'll go," said Johnny.

"Wait, Johnny!" Mary kicked her horse around in front
of the sorrel. "I don't know who those two men were back
there in the saloon, but they're up to no good. I'll get the
license while you wait here and keep out of sight."

He dropped the sorrel's reins on the ground and went
into the church. It was plain and unadorned, with a few
rows of battered benches. He was still carrying his hat,
and he paced up and down the aisle, watching for Mary,
apprehensive for any sign of Mason and Lem. If they
guessed who he was, they'd be after him.

Mary returned with the license, but she was worried
too. "Those two men were arguing in the street about you,
Johnny. They're both drunk!"

Johnny asked nervously, "Where is Clark?"

"The woman said—"

He was beginning to sweat. "She said he'd be here right away. We ain't got all day! Where is he?"

"Johnny, are you scared of those two men?"

He gulped. "Why should I be?"

"You did something to them," she guessed.

"They forced me to," he said.

"What was it?"

"A fight."

"With guns?"

"No, just a regular fight."

"I'm glad," she said.

He whirled on her. "Glad of what?"

"That it wasn't guns."

"If it had been," he muttered, "they wouldn't be lookin' for me now."

"Johnny," she said presently, "why does a man change?"

"Change? How?"

"Today I've been thinking about you and me, Johnny. I've been remembering when I first saw you."

"You were a kid then," said Johnny.

"Yes—and you were not much more. I remember how you were when you rode into town with your brother." She looked up at him. "I loved you right away, Johnny. You were different then."

Johnny shook his head. "No different—just younger, that's all."

"Why does a man change, Johnny?"

"Do you mean what makes a man a coward?" He turned on one heel. "Do you mean why I am walkin' up and down sweatin' blood at the thought of those two coyotes out there after me?"

She looked at the floor.

"I don't think a man really changes," he said. "Sometimes it takes a while and a lot of different things happening to bring out what he's like—but inside he was that way all the time, only it didn't show. I was a bully as long as I had Red's guns behind me. When Tallman killed him, that was the end of me."

"Not the end, Johnny. The beginning. You never had

a chance before. Red kept you under this thumb; he told you what to do and you did it. But now it's different. Now you can make your own way; you can work out your own life."

He shook his head slowly. "From what's been happening, I'd say it isn't working out too well, Mary."

He could see she was bewildered at fighting this thing that was within him. He was bewildered himself. He stood before her, and saw the tears streaming down her face. He leaned down to touch her and heard a voice call:

"Hey, you!"

He turned. Dan Mason said, "Get away from her!"

Johnny moved a couple of steps.

"Ain't you Johnny Concho?" asked Mason.

Johnny saw the six-shooter in Mason's holster, and he was frightened. He saw the hatred in Mason's eyes, and he was afraid his knees would buckle.

He tried to answer, but he couldn't open his mouth. He felt like a trapped wolf. He was caught and he couldn't move, and every way he turned somebody was looking for him with a gun. He stared from Mason to Lem and back to Mary, and sweat stood out on the backs of his hands.

"I said are you Johnny Concho under all those bandages!" Mason insisted.

Johnny swallowed. "No. No, I'm not," he said.

He saw Mary's eyes close.

Mason growled. "I don't believe you." He started toward Johnny. "I'm sayin' you're Johnny Concho. You may be afraid to admit it, but you're Johnny Concho."

"No," whispered Johnny.

"It ain't Red, is it?" asked Lem.

"Red is dead."

Johnny looked for a way to escape, but Lem had the door barred.

Mason put a hand on his gun butt. "I'm gonna find out if that's real blood on them bandages."

A booming voice said: "Mr. Mason, take off your hat in the house of God."

Barney Clark, his white hair standing out in the dimness inside the church, was coming from somewhere near the pulpit. A pearl-handled pistol hung at his hip.

"This ain't none of your affair, Barney," said Mason.

Clark answered coldly, "I said take off your hat."

Lem took off his hat.

Clark said, "Lem has a better memory than you, Mr. Mason."

Lem said hastily, "I didn't come lookin' for no trouble with you, Barney."

Clark turned to Mason. "Are you willing to draw your pistol with a servant of the Lord? You have three seconds. One, two—"

Mason, scowling, took off his hat.

Clark smiled. "That's better. Now that that is over, I will ask you and your friend to leave while this young couple is united in holy matrimony."

Mason said stubbornly, "I got business with this feller."

Clark said, "You've got business with Johnny Concho. I heard this man identified otherwise."

"He's lyin'," said Mason.

Clark looked at Johnny. "What is your name, young man?"

"Jones—John Jones."

Mason snorted. "Why, you—"

Clark said in a hard voice, "Good day, Mr. Mason."

The two men left, but Mason turned at the door: "I'll be waitin' for you, Johnny Concho."

Clark smiled. "Now, shall we proceed with the ceremony?"

Johnny nodded and held out his hand to Mary, but to his astonishment she shook her head.

"No, Johnny. I'm sorry. I wanted you because I loved you. I knew you were mixed up, but I thought I wanted you anyway. I was wrong."

"Mary, please—"

"What I thought I loved," she said, "has changed—or it wasn't there in the first place. I thought when you got away from Red's influence, you'd be different. But now you—you aren't the boy who rode into Cripple Creek three years ago. I know you've been beaten terribly, Johnny, and I can't stand the thought of any more of it. But, Johnny—" she was crying now—"I can't marry a man who doesn't have enough pride to defend his own name."

She left the church. Johnny stood there, stunned. Finally he turned to Clark and said, "She was the only one who ever believed in me."

"Sit down, young man." Clark's voice was gentle.

Johnny sat in one of the battered pews. "When I go out there," he said, "they'll be waiting for me. What will happen then? Will I crawl—or will I get a chance to crawl?"

"You're asking for help in the house of the Lord," Clark said. "I don't know that you came here for that purpose, but you're in that house and you're asking for help. Maybe we can work something out."

"I could use some help," Johnny admitted.

"Tell me who you are."

Johnny said grimly, "Johnny Concho."

"Then go home, Johnny Concho."

"Be brave, I suppose?"

"Yes."

"It ain't easy."

Clark nodded as if to himself. "Then Mason was right."

"That I'm yellow?" Johnny said bitterly. "They'll tell you that all over Arizona."

"Listen, Johnny. What makes you think you're yellow?"

"Because I don't want to fight with guns."

"In your opinion, does gunfighting make a man a brave man?"

"That's the way it looks."

"You're quite wrong, Johnny. The bravest deed I have ever seen was done by a man who wore two guns, but he didn't use either of them."

"Maybe he was afraid to draw."

"Most people undoubtedly think so. And yet he did something that took far more courage—he walked into the face of another man's gun when he didn't know whether or not he could draw his own. And when he found out he could not draw, he didn't run. He stood there and took the worst pistol-whipping a man ever took in Arizona." The reverend was talking excitedly. "I damn near— I almost forgot myself and interfered—but I am glad now I did not."

"Why?"

"Because I never would have had the chance to teach you this great lesson."

Johnny frowned. "But when a man is waitin' for you, like them two out there—"

"Johnny, did you know Red very well—the last few years, I mean."

"I saw him once in a while."

"You always admired Red, didn't you?"

"He took care of me when I was little."

Clark nodded slowly. "In every man there must be one spot of goodness, one soft place that the Lord can touch and call His own. That must have been the way with Red. His one soft spot was you, Johnny."

"What do you mean by that, Reverend?"

"I've known Red many years, Johnny, and I say to you that his soft spot for you was the only one he ever had! Johnny, he was not a man for you to pattern yourself after. Other men's wives, like Pearl Lang; dictatorships over towns like Cripple Creek; and killings—cold, bloody killings that he always managed to get out of. He wasn't a brave man, Johnny. He was a coward; that's why he depended on guns."

Johnny swallowed hard. "You mean—you knew Red —and he was—no good?"

Clark said, "He was a coward, a sneak and a murderer. I'm sorry."

"You lie!" said Johnny.

Clark said coldly, "Hold your tongue!"

"You lie! My brother wasn't scared of any man that ever lived."

"Then why did he use guns? Why does Tallman use guns? If Tallman is not afraid, why doesn't he go into Cripple Creek and try to make a living like anybody else? Take his gun away and he will be a coward like your brother."

"Shut your mouth!" Johnny cried, rising.

Clark stood up. "Would you fight me, Johnny Concho?"

Johnny shouted, "I'll kill you!"

He leaped for Clark, who in one smooth motion whipped out his pistol and laid the muzzle against Johnny's stomach. Johnny froze. Clark looked at him for a moment, then slowly turned the gun around and extended it to Johnny, butt first. "Take my weapon," he said quietly, "and see if the feel of vengeance can cleanse your soul. You have it in your power to kill me, Johnny Concho, if you think murder will answer your need."

Johnny lowered his head suddenly. "What'll I do?" he asked brokenly.

"I think you'd better go home, Johnny."

Johnny looked up. "I don't understand. Sometimes a gun is the only answer. Why?"

"Because," said Clark, "evil men take advantage of peaceful persons to enforce their will. Yes, Johnny, unfortunately you are right—but there is a difference between an occasional use of guns in true self-defense and a habitual use in aggression."

"I don't want to kill," said Johnny.

"I have seen that." Clark nodded wisely. "You have not the killer instinct. A man is either a killer or he is not a killer, and there is nothing he can do to change it. You are not a killer, Johnny. That is why you could not draw against Duke Lang. You thought you ought to, because you knew that's what Red would have done, but in your heart you weren't a killer and so you took a whipping rather than draw."

"Then you don't think I'm a coward?"

"Positively not. Afraid, yes. Only a fool is not afraid. But a coward—no."

"I'm listenin'," said Johnny. "For the first time in my life I'm listenin'."

"The power is not in the gun, Johnny. The power is ultimately in the man behind it. A gun is a tool. It is a man who pulls the trigger—a man with determination, or a man in defense of himself or his loved ones—or even a man with fear. The power is in the man."

Johnny looked at him a long time. Finally he said slowly, "I'm goin' back home."

Clark said, "Mason and Lem may try to change your mind."

Johnny said, "I'll take that chance."

Clark looked at his pearl-handled pistol. "Here lies the spirit of evil, but the path of righteousness must be found." He smiled. "I will lead you to that path." He spun the pistol on his forefinger and chucked it into the holster. He started out of the church with Johnny close behind him.

He caught up a horse to ride back through town with Johnny. On the other side of town, Mason and Lem rode out from behind a boulder. Clark and Johnny stopped.

"All right, Reverend," said Mason. "We ain't in your house now. Step aside."

Clark motioned for Johnny to go ahead. Johnny moved the sorrel, and Clark followed.

Mason said stubbornly, "I'm warnin' you, Barney."

Johnny rode on past. Clark followed him for a few feet, then turned his horse to face the two men. "Unfortunately," he said, "there are no scriptures to cover this situation, so I'll say, Dan Mason, that if you touch that gun you're a dead man!"

Mason sucked in a deep breath. He looked at Johnny and he glowered at Clark, but the reverend didn't budge. His booming voice rose in the valley: "The Lord be with you, Johnny Concho!"

Johnny reached a rise in the road. He turned to look back at the reverend, then pushed the sorrel into a lope. He was going home—and home to him was Cripple Creek. Cripple Creek needed somebody to lead it in its fight against Tallman. Perhaps, at long last, Johnny Concho would be that man.

Chapter Seventeen

JOHNNY STOPPED at the next town and found a doctor. He asked first how far he was from Rawhide.

"Next town," the doctor said. "You want to wait until you get there?"

"No," said Johnny. "I want these bandages off."

"They'll be stuck a little," the doctor said, looking at his watch, "and they'll hurt. Why don't you go out and get a couple of drinks first?"

"Not a bad idea." He went outside. The sorrel was standing there switching flies. Johnny took a look at the gaunt barrel and bony hips, and looked up and down the street until he saw a livery. He rode the sorrel in and arranged for a good feed of oats. Before leaving he took the $300 from the saddlebag and put it inside of his shirt. Then he went into the Gray Rooster Saloon and asked for a drink.

"Anything special?" asked the bartender.

"What have you got?"

The bartender turned back quickly and leaned over. "The best whisky this side of Holbrook," he said eagerly. "Old Lightning. Costs twenty cents a drink, though."

"I can stand it," said Johnny.

The bartender reached behind the other bottles and raised a smaller bottle shaped like a barrel cactus. "It's as soft as a baby's kiss," he said, "but it sort of creeps up on you."

"Pour three," said Johnny. "Right here."

"Mister," the bartender said reproachfully, "this whisky should be drunk slowly and savored."

Johnny looked at him and said reassuringly, "I'll savor it. Just you shovel it out."

By the time he got back to the doctor's office he felt ready for anything. For a while he didn't think he'd be able to sit in the chair, and he seemed to keep floating up while the doctor was softening the bandages with water. But when the man ripped off the first strip of gauze it brought him back to earth. His fingers clamped around the arms of the chair.

"You're a truthful man, doc." He thought of the bartender, and realized that only now the Old Lightning was beginning to hit bottom. "This is a truthful town," he said. "There ought to be more like it."

"We had a good mayor once," said the doctor. "He set the pattern for the town. It's been a good town ever since."

"Where's your mayor now?" asked Johnny.

"Up in the cemetery."

Johnny stared at him. "Ain't there any way to be good and stay alive at the same time?"

"Oh, it wasn't that so much." The doctor ripped off another strip of gauze, and Johnny held on as the room floated back and forth around him like a pendulum. "It was a private fight, you might say."

Johnny grunted.

"Fellow named Joe Helgeson—best blacksmith we ever had in this town. Both good men, but they disagreed. The mayor took a notion to a gold-trimmed saddle Helgeson was making, and insisted on buying it from him. Helgeson wouldn't sell, and one thing led to another." The doctor moistened a spot just under Johnny's right eye. "You know how those things go."

"Yeah," said Johnny. "Joe Helgeson, eh?"

"You know him?"

"I thought maybe I did," Johnny said thoughtfully, "but now I'm wondering if it was somebody else. Helgeson shot him?"

"Yes—quite dead. Helgeson was known as a dead shot. I never knew what happened to Helgeson. Some folks thought the killing unnerved him. Anyway, he swore never to touch a gun again, and moved on. The mayor was his sister's husband, you see."

Johnny shook his head slowly.

"Am I hurting you much, mister?"

Johnny said, "Not too much. Not quite enough." He sat back for a moment. "Ever hear of Cripple Creek?"

"Enough to know where it is; that's about all. We get our supplies from Holbrook. Cripple Creek is over the mountains and in the next county, and it's hardly more than a name to us. It could as well be in California."

"If you swore never to touch a gun," said Johnny, "and

your town was taken over by a couple of badmen, what would you do?"

"That's a hard question to answer—unless you want to get killed."

"That's what I figured," Johnny said, sitting back.

A while later the doctor said, "That'll do you for now. I'd suggest leaving the bandages off for a few days to give the wounds a chance to heal. Will you be around our town for a while?"

"How long will it take, doc, for the cuts to grow back together?"

"Not very long. They're healing well but still tender, of course. Not entirely closed yet. I'd—"

"Got a hotel here?"

"Right across the street. The stage comes in every morning at ten-ten."

"How much do I owe you?"

"One dollar—if that's all right."

"All right?"

"It must have hurt quite a bit," the doctor said apologetically.

"Doc," said Johnny, "I been hurt ten times that bad and nobody even said go to hell." He planted a silver dollar in the doctor's hand, and went to find a room. He wanted to look a little better for Mary—provided she would look at him. Right now the red marks of the cuts down his face were not much better than the strips of court plaster.

He stayed for a couple of days, thinking it over, soaking up the Arizona sun, sleeping in it, gathering energy. At the end he still didn't know the answer: what to do, how to do it, when to do it, or whether he would have the courage when it came to a showdown. But at least he would go back and find out.

Milo came in that day on the stage from Holbrook, and was astonished to find him sitting in the sun. "I take it you've shook the dust of Cripple Creek from your feet for good, Johnny."

Johnny stirred lazily. "Anybody else take it that way?"

"Just about everybody, I guess." Milo untwisted a trace strap and rehooked it in the singletree. "Doggone that hostler. I told him he'd ought to use a lantern to harness up by."

"You make the run through Cripple Creek any more?"

"Every other week."

"How are they gettin' along with Tallman?"

Milo straightened up. "Not so good. You know what happened? Albert Dark said he'd rather have *you* there."

Johnny sat forward on the edge of the chair. "Meaning what?"

"Well, I—" Milo floundered. "Peace of mind, I reckon."

Johnny sat back, and the driver went into the hotel. "All aboard for Mountain Junction!" he called. "We'll stop there for dinner."

Two persons got onto the stage, and Milo picked up a deflated mailbag. "So long, Johnny," he said.

Johnny sat back. "So long, Milo." He pulled his hat low over his eyes and thought about it, there in the warm sun. It was about time for him to move on, it looked as if.

He rode out the next morning, letting the sorrel take its time. He cut across Sam Green's pasture and had something to eat. Sam seemed to have forgotten all his grievances against Johnny in the new situation with Tallman.

"It's a bad thing," Sam said, watching his plate as he speared a piece of meat with his knife. "Cripple Creek is worse off than ever."

"Sam!" said his wife. "Use your fork!"

He looked at her, finally comprehending what she meant, sighed, and picked up his fork.

"It's worse than—me and Red?" asked Johnny.

"A lot. With you and Red we had to kick in, but it wasn't too much. We thought then it was, but we found out better. Anyway, Johnny, you weren't such a bad one. You acted a little biggety, but we never really figured you for a badman. With Tallman, now, it's different. He wears them guns and he's a killer; you can see it in his eyes."

"What makes a killer?" asked Johnny.

Sam looked at him absently. "A fellow that doesn't give a damn about anybody else, and that ain't got sense enough to be afraid."

"Isn't Henderson doing anything?"

"No—and maybe I don't blame him—though I've spoken my mind to him about it. Henderson is paid to keep the peace."

"And to risk his life, if Cripple Creek needs it," said his gray-haired wife.

Sam argued. "I don't agree with that, Viola. No man is paid to die. No man is paid to risk his life except in a war, and I don't figure Pete Henderson has got any more call to have a showdown with Tallman than the rest of us. It's just as much our duty to fight Tallman as it is Pete's."

"You're forgetting something, Sam," she said. "Pete Henderson is used to handling guns, and he's used to men like Tallman."

Sam's answer was positive. "He's too old for that—anyway he never was good enough in the first place." He looked at Johnny. "I was camped outside of Abilene with a trail-herd," he said, "in the summer of Seventy-three. The grasshoppers was terrible in Kansas, and there wasn't no market for beef, and the Jayhawkers was hollerin' their heads off about Texas fever. We had been there over a month, day-herdin' the cattle and tryin' to keep them on grass without crossin' any plowed furrows —there wasn't no bobwire that year—and somebody organized a posse to chase us back to Texas. We weren't doin' no harm. A few of the boys would slip off to town and ride up an' down the street and unload their pistols once in a while, but hell, they had been on the trail for months! They weren't hurtin' anybody. Anyway," he went on in a lower voice, "this posse come. It mighta been Jay-hawkers. I don't know. I always suspected it was organized by outlaws who wanted to scatter my herd so they could round them up later for themselves. Course I never had no use for Jayhawkers, but a lot of the deviltry laid to them was started by somebody else."

Johnny pushed his hat back. "Where did Pete come in?"

Sam blinked. "Oh! Pete showed up with one deputy. They both had sawed-off shotguns. They faced down them outlaws and run 'em off—and Pete was drygulched on the way back to town. Three bullets in his back. Laid in bed for four months."

Johnny said in a low voice: "I never knew that."

Sam Green went on as if talking to himself. "The West was built like that—by a lot of men who did things that was forgotten the next day because worse things come along. Once in a while you hear about them—like Billy Tilghman, maybe, or Bat Masterson. But mostly they're either buried and forgotten or they go off and take up in some small town and hope they don't have to face anymore gunslingin' artists. Do you know—" he pointed his knife at Johnny—"that Pete Henderson can't raise his right arm higher'n his belt?"

"I remember now," Johnny said thoughtfully. "Doc Murchison gave him that."

"Sam!" said his wife. "The knife!"

"Yes'm." Sam laid down the knife.

"I'd forgot that," Johnny said soberly.

"No call to talk about it," said Sam Green. "Coffee ready, Viola?"

She poured it, and Sam sat there stirring with the handle of his fork. "Tallman is gettin' under my skin," he said.

"Now, Sam—"

"He's also goin' to break me by next spring if something isn't done."

"Sam Green!" his wife said. "I don't want you getting any young ideas. You aren't no snortin' youngster any more."

"I've got my pride," said Sam.

"You can't gunfight Tallman," said Johnny. "He outdrew my brother."

"Guns?" Sam Green looked thoughtful. "No, I wouldn't try. I've got something stronger—my will."

"Yes," said his wife. "That's got a lot of good men killed."

"Maybe. It's also made the way a little smoother for them that was left."

Johnny rode on toward Cripple Creek. It was not until long after dark that he saw the shadowed cluster of buildings below that marked the town. He walked the sorrel down out of the hills to Helgeson's blacksmith shop. Long before he got there he heard the ringing of iron on iron as Helgeson worked at his anvil. He rode up to the open door and got down and walked in.

"Hello, Helgeson," he said.

Joe stopped his hammering for a moment and looked at Johnny, studied him, thought about it, and returned to his work. "Ping, ping—bong! Ping, ping—bong!" He always bounced the hammer twice on the anvil to get the feel of it.

"Like to put up my horse," said Johnny.

Helgeson motioned with his head, not looking up. His body, naked from the waist up, was dirty from the day's work. "Same stall, same price." He hit the iron viciously. "But not the same service."

Johnny didn't answer. He led his horse through the blacksmith shop and into the corral. He took off the saddle and blanket and threw them on the top plank of the partition that made up the side of the stall. He rubbed the sorrel with dry straw, forked some hay from overhead, and measured out a quart of oats in the worn, shallow wooden box in one corner. He closed the gate behind the sorrel and went back to the blacksmith shop. "I see you've still got the gold saddle," he said, walking over to it.

Helgeson looked up. "I've got it," he said grumpily, "and I'm keeping it. Tallman wants it as much as you did, but that's one thing I'm not giving up."

"I understand," said Johnny.

Helgeson glowered at him as much as to say that he doubted that Johnny had ever understood anything. "He'll get that saddle over my dead body," he said.

Johnny fingered the filigree work, then took off his bandanna and polished the marks his fingers had left. "Mrs. Brown still keep roomers?" he asked.

"When there is one."

Johnny walked down the street almost to the Copper Diggin's, then turned right and went to Mrs. Brown's house. He knocked, and Mrs. Brown came to the door with a lamp in her hand. "Johnny Concho!" she exclaimed.

"Yes, ma'am. I'm lookin' for a room."

"Well, I always say—" her voice was high and flat— "that a bad penny comes home to roost." She looked hard at his face, "You've got money, haven't you?"

"Enough to pay for a room," said Johnny.

"No meals included," she warned.

"I can eat at Bennie's."

"Then come in." She looked at his blanket roll. "I hope you haven't got any critters in those blankets. How about your shoes?" She sniffed. "Just come out of the corral, didn't you?"

"Yes, ma'am. I rubbed them off in the dirt."

"Come along."

It was a small room, very ordinary, but he could sleep there until he could decide what to do about Tallman—or until Tallman found out he was in Cripple Creek and reminded him that he had been ordered out of town. Only then, Johnny knew, would he himself find out what he was inside. He no longer had Red behind him; he had no guns. What did he have to fight with? Pride? It took him down a notch to think about it.

From what Barney Clark had said—and this had been supported, he now realized, by a hundred things others had said in the past weeks—Red Concho had not been a brother a man could be proud of. Johnny still had a soft spot in his heart for him, because Red had taken care of him—maybe not in the best way, but the best Red knew—and Johnny would have fought for him without a second thought. But this was a different story. There was no Red, and nothing to fight for—but pride, maybe. Pride in restoring respectability to the family name, pride in his own name, pride in all the things that went to make up a man. Johnny had that pride, but was it strong enough? Would he back down at the last minute, as he had always done before? There was no way to know without trying.

The next morning he had breakfast at Bennie's. "Nice to see you, Mr. Concho," said Bennie. "Eggs or steak this morning?"

"Eggs," said Johnny. "With ham."

"Yes, sir." Bennie raised a stove lid and thrust in a chunk of pine. "You just going through, Mr. Concho?"

"You can call me Johnny—and I don't know whether I'm just going through or whether I'm going to stay."

He went into Albert Dark's general store, that still smelled of pickles and stock tonic. "Morning, Mr. Dark."

"Johnny! How are you!" He came from behind the laden-down counter and looked at Johnny's face, shaking his head. "It was an awful thing," he said.

"It's over," said Johnny.

"It was magnificent," said Dark. "I never saw anything like it. I wish," said Dark, "that I were a man of violence. I would like to do something glorious—something dramatic—just once."

"Where is Mary?" asked Johnny.

"She is not in to you, young man," Sarah Dark said ominously from the curtain.

Johnny flinched, but he said, "I'd like to speak to her, if you don't mind."

"She's getting a pail of water."

Johnny went through the parted curtains, through the kitchen with its good smell of baking, into the back yard, where he stood on the step and listened to the rusty screeching of the pump. Mary made quite a picture as she worked the handle, and Johnny took time to appreciate it. She was wearing a calico dress that almost brushed the ground but fitted her very snugly from the waist up, and had a small white collar that set off her black hair, which was glossy and gleaming in the sun.

He walked quietly up behind her and laid his fingers over her hand. She stopped pumping abruptly, turned to stare at him, said, "Oh, Johnny!" and then suddenly remembered and said in a quieter voice: "Hello, Johnny."

That sobered him. He took his hand away from hers. "Hello, Mary."

She was scrutinizing his face. "You—took the bandages off."

"The doc said I didn't need them any more."

"I'm glad."

"Mary!" He pulled her to him. "You can't stand off at long range like this!"

"I don't know you, Johnny," she said.

His arms dropped. "Mary, I want you to know you're the one, all right; there never has been anybody but you."

Her lips parted and he saw her eyes soften in surrender, but abruptly she caught herself. "Sorry, Johnny. This is baking day, and I have to fill the reservoir on the stove. I'll see you around—if you stay."

If he stayed. A lot depended on his staying. But how did a man without guns stay in a town that had a man like Tallman—and stay alive?

He carried the bucket into the kitchen for her, and went back into the store. Yes, he thought as he parted the curtains, it was something of a problem. Probably Tallman already knew he was in town, and Tallman would have to give the same verdict: "Run or draw." And there was nothing to draw.

He heard a familiar voice talking to Albert: "Mr. Tallman has called a meeting for tonight, Al. Wants everybody there at eight o'clock sharp."

"What for?" asked Albert.

"He didn't say."

Albert moved from behind his counter. "We can't possibly answer any more demands, Mr. Henderson. We are paying the limit as it is."

"If you got any ideas about it," Henderson said shortly, "you better tell them to Tallman tonight."

Johnny stepped out. "Hello, Sheriff."

Chapter Eighteen

Henderson looked him over. "I see you're back," he said flatly.

"Yes."

Henderson looked more closely at the healing scabs on Johnny's face. "Looks like you've seen some of the world."

"A little."

"Where you headed?"

"To the Copper Diggin's."

"I'll go part-way with you."

"Thanks."

"Tallman is up to Silver City this morning, so there won't be any trouble from him until nightfall."

"What's he doing in Silver City?"

"Lookin' at the mines."

"A big outfit," Johnny observed as they started up the dusty street facing the distant mountains.

"So I heard—but it would get him off *our* back."

"And leave Cripple Creek wide open for somebody else to move in?"

Henderson grunted. He turned in at his office. "You better stay out of sight tonight when Tallman gets back," he said.

Johnny nodded. The sheriff had cast his vote. Johnny went on to the saloon and walked inside. His boot heels made hollow sounds on the board floor. "Pour me a drink, Harry," he said.

Harry stared at him. "It's fifteen cents," he said hastily.

"Give me some of that twenty-cent stuff you keep special." Johnny dropped a silver dollar on the bar and watched it vibrate until it settled down. He raised the glass and saw someone behind him. He turned to face Duke Lang.

Duke glanced at his waist. "Still afraid," he sneered.

Johnny said coldly, "Didn't you get the satisfaction you wanted?"

Surprisingly, Duke's reaction was not triumph but bleakness. "I gave you what was coming to you," he said.

"Then shut up!" Johnny said.

Duke backed a step. "I'm not afraid of you," he said. "You showed yourself a coward. But that's no affair of mine, for I'm not running Cripple Creek. Tallman is running this town, and it's him you'll have to answer to."

Johnny looked at the glass of whisky. "I figured that out," he said quietly, "a long time ago."

"You didn't come here to pick a fight with me?" Duke asked warily.

Johnny tossed off the drink. "No," he said.

Duke stared at him. Finally he said, "All right." Johnny watched Harry go to the kitchen, and turned around. "I think I know how you felt," he said, "and I'm sorry—but I want to tell you one thing, Duke: what you thought about me and Pearl wasn't so."

Duke glared at him. "The hell it wasn't!"

Johnny shook his head. "No, sir, it was not. She followed because she was interested in some mining options and she needed somebody to travel with. That's as far as it went."

Duke took a deep breath. "If I could believe you—"

"You've got no reason not to."

"Except—" Duke obviously was keeping his voice level with great effort. "Except Pearl didn't come back."

Johnny didn't answer. He had just realized why Pearl had lied to him and told him that Red was not dead: to keep him in Silver City until she could get her hands on the options. Maybe it was just as good for Duke that she had not come back.

Johnny was sitting at a table in the saloon that evening when the stage came in. He heard the screeching of the brake, the rattling of the coach, the groaning of wood, the jingling of trace chains, and he knew that Milo was at the reins and handling things with his usual flourish. He sat there gripping his glass and trying to calm the excitement and apprehension inside of him while he waited for the passengers. A man entered the door, and Johnny started, but it wasn't Tallman; it was Eccles. Behind him was Benson; following him was Pearson. They registered and got rooms, while Johnny watched the door and waited,

his stomach feeling hollower and hollower. Then Milo
came in and hollered, "Anybody for Holbrook?" and
picked up the mailbag.

Johnny asked, "Any other passengers?"

"Nope. That's the ticket." Milo's eyes widened when
he looked at Johnny. "You sure move around, boy."

Johnny nodded, the tension beginning to ease off a little.
"I've got a good horse," he said.

Albert Dark and Joe Helgeson came in for the meeting
Henderson had announced. Albert looked sheepish, Joe
truculent. They went over to the bar for a drink, and
Eccles, already there, turned to greet them. "Good evening, gentlemen!" he boomed. "Mind if I buy the first
one?"

Helgeson glowered at him suspiciously, but Dark
nodded.

Eccles introduced himself. "I'm looking for options,"
he said.

Albert Dark looked blank. "Options?"

"Sure, options on mining claims. There's nothing spec-
tacular, of course, but the company likes to get all these
little things cleaned up and out of the way—and I am told
that there are some options held in Cripple Creek."

Johnny saw Dark's hand go involuntarily to his hip
pocket. Dark looked at him, but Johnny shook his head.
It was too early in the game to show their hole card. If the
president of Amalgamated had come all the way from
Silver City, he hadn't come just to pick up some nuisance
claims for a few dollars. He wanted that eight-thousand-
dollar claim that Pearl had wanted to sell him, and he had
persuaded Pearl to tell him about it before she left, by
invitation, for California. Under the circumstances, if it
had been worth eight thousand then, it was worth every
cent of eight thousand now. He decided to check, and let
Eccles do the betting.

Albert Dark's mouth opened, but again he looked at
Johnny, and again Johnny shook his head. Finally Albert
swallowed and said, "Well, we aren't much of an invest-
ing town, Mr. Eccles."

Johnny got up and walked across the floor. "There might
be a few options stashed away, Mr. Eccles, but it'll take
time to dig them out. Anyway, you'll be here tomorrow.

You can't very well leave until tomorrow noon—unless you rent a rig."

"I'm not in that big a hurry," said Eccles, obviously playing a close game. "I'll stay overnight and look your town over. It may be that Amalgamated can use a nice little town like this."

"This town is bein' used already," Helgeson said harshly.

Eccles turned to him. "What do you mean by that, sir?"

"He means," said Dark, "that the future of Cripple Creek is very bright at this moment."

"Nice to find such great town spirit," said Eccles, and looked at Johnny. "Young man, haven't I seen you before? Weren't you—"

"Sure!" Benson spoke up excitedly. "He's the gent who—"

Johnny saw Duke, at the desk, look up. "Sure," Johnny said quickly, "I was the gent who held four kings to your—"

"No," said Benson firmly. "No, you saw my—"

"Gents!" said Johnny loudly. "Step up and have a drink on me!"

Albert Dark raised his glass. There were many questions in his eyes, but Johnny shook his head.

Benson put down his glass. "Now, young man, I want to straighten out this business about the poker game. It was you, Mr. Eccles, who held the full house, and it was I—"

Johnny wanted desperately to head off the conversation, for it was only a matter of seconds until somebody would remember Pearl—for she was the kind a man would remember—and mention her, and then Duke Lang would know what a no-good she was, and once again his pride would be back in the dirt. But Johnny couldn't think of anything more to say.

At that moment, however, a gravelly voice came from the door: "Evenin', gents. Glad to see you're all gatherin' early for my little meetin'."

He turned to face Tallman.

Tallman looked them over, and his eyes lifted when he saw Johnny. He seemed to consider this development for a moment. He glanced at Johnny's waist, and then back at his face. "I'll take care of you later," he said. Obviously he wanted time to think.

He went upstairs, and Johnny saw that the saloon was pretty well filled. Sam Green, Judge Tyler, Joe Helgeson, Albert Dark, and a number of others were standing together in the far corner, and Johnny went over to them.

Helgeson said, "Maybe we ought to wait for the sheriff."

Tyler said, "Pete Henderson won't change anything."

"He might have some ideas," said Albert Dark. "Something that's been done before—in Abilene, maybe, or Dodge City."

Joe Helgeson said glumly, "Sure, it's been done before —but who'll do it here?"

"Mr. Tallman has his own set of rules," said Tyler. "I doubt that we shall be able to find any precedent."

Sam Green said, "We've got to figure something out— not just talk."

"Talk is better than getting killed, Sam."

Albert sighed.

Tyler said, "Sam, maybe if we go along with him for a while he'll cool off and then we'll be able to talk some sense into him."

Sam said impatiently, "Yeah, maybe if we get down on our knees he'll give us permission to live. Is that the way you want to keep on?" He glared at them all.

Joe Helgeson muttered something.

Tyler, careful to keep his voice low, said, "Still best to think things out, Sam."

Sam said angrily, "I did my thinking after he sent his partner out to my ranch."

"I have been visited too," said Albert Dark.

"Me too," growled Helgeson.

"You gents got nothin' to complain about," said Bennie. "I'm supposed to give him and Walker free meals."

"He told me," said Sam, "how much he expects to get when I sell a herd of cattle. Demanded to see my bills of lading even! He'll bleed us dry, I tell you."

"This kind of man is restless," said Tyler. "In a month or so he'll probably move along. We'll wake up some morning and find he's ridden out."

"You're full of hot air," said Sam Green. "You're

tryin' to hide from the truth. Well, not Sam Green! Not
any longer. I say we run him out now!"

"How?" asked Tyler.

Sam Green's eyes narrowed and his jaw hardened. "A
gun is the only thing he understands. That's the only way
to talk to him. How many are with me?"

He looked around, but there was no answer. They all
looked at the floor.

Sam demanded: "I said, how many are with me?"

And again came that gravelly voice: "It looks like you're
all alone, Sam Green."

The men turned together. Sam looked belligerent; Albert Dark seemed to gasp for breath; Helgeson looked re-
sentful; Bennie was scared.

Sam said, "This has always been a peaceful town, Tallman."

Tallman hooked his thumbs in his belt and walked toward them, swaying. "I aim to keep it that way," he
said.

But Sam Green didn't scare. "We say get out of Cripple
Creek! Pack up your gear and ride."

"You say we," said Tallman, "but I don't hear nobody's
voice but yours."

"These men are all with me," Sam said. "We have
agreed that this isn't the town for you or anybody like
you!"

Tallman turned his back on Sam and said to the others:
"I've got papers and deeds—things for all of you to sign.
We got to have it legal, don't we, Judge?"

Tyler said slowly, "If that's the way you want it. But
a paper signed under duress—"

Tallman's voice ground out: "That's the way I want
it!"

Sam Green said, "Well, I don't." He spoke to the men.
"The rest of you can crawl—but not Sam Green. I cleared
this land—and so did you, Judge Tyler, when you was
readin' law—and so did you, Bennie, when you was home-
steadin'—and so did you, Joe Helgeson, when you come to
work in the timber. We broke our backs for this land,
and I ain't goin' to hand it over to any man at the point
of a gun." He glared at Tallman and started to walk
away.

Tallman said quietly, "Sam Green."

Sam spun as if his name had been called in a gunfight. "Don't Sam Green me!" he shouted. "I'm goin' for my rifle!"

Tallman said, "I calculate that's a threat."

"That's exactly what it is," said Sam. "When I come back with that rifle you'd better be on your horse or I start shootin'." He glared at Tallman, looked at the others, then turned and continued toward the door.

He made it halfway, and then there was a shot, and Sam grunted as the bullet struck him. Johnny looked at Tallman. Smoke was rising around his face. He replaced his gun in its holster and looked around. "Like Sam Green figured," he said slowly, "this is a peaceful town and we don't want no trouble." He paused. "Do we?" Nobody answered. "I'll have the papers for you to sign in a few minutes," he said.

Helgeson looked at Sam Green's body on the floor. Helgeson's weathered face was white, and he dropped to his knees beside Green's body and pushed a big hand inside his shirt.

Tyler stared at Tallman. "That's murder," he said incredulously.

Tallman turned. "You heard him say he was comin' back with a rifle, didn't you? It was self-defense."

Albert Dark stared down at Sam's body, and then at the men around him as if in reproach. A hardness came over his face that Johnny never had seen there. He walked straight to the door and went out.

Tallman watched him sardonically; he didn't try to stop him. He walked easily to the bar and said, "Give me a drink, Harry."

Eccles stared at him a moment and then moved a step farther away.

Helgeson shook his head. He picked the body up in his arms and carried it out. Pete Henderson was just outside, and he watched Helgeson move slowly, heavily, like a man in a death march. Then he came in and looked at Tyler. Tallman had gone back upstairs. "Was it him?"

Tyler said harshly, "It was Tallman. He called it self-defense—in the back."

Johnny said slowly, "I sat at Sam Green's table yesterday with him and his wife. Sam treated me like a man." He looked into their eyes. "Now he's dead. How is Mrs. Green going to feel when they bring him home over the road he made with a grubbing hoe and an ax?" He looked at Henderson and at Tyler. "We've got to face down Tallman and run him out of the country!"

Tyler shook his head. "You don't know the whole story, Johnny. Tallman got everybody to give him a share in their business when he first came here."

"A share!"

"Yes. He wanted just a small share—a hundred dollars, say, and for that he would protect everybody in Cripple Creek from any gunslinger who might show up. Everybody went along, thinking it would be the last demand and they were lucky to get off that easy. But it was only the beginning, Johnny. He produced partnership contracts for everybody to sign, and they looked innocent enough, but by the time I got a chance to examine them I found that every man who had signed such a contract had also signed an agreement not to sell his business without agreement of the other partner—Tallman. So," he went on wearily, "what can Albert Dark do, for instance? He can up and leave, but he can't take his store or his goods with him. Tallman won't let him go, and Tallman won't let him sell out. What's a poor devil like Dark going to do, Johnny?"

Johnny said, "He's making you sign over still more, isn't he?"

"Profit-sharing agreements—to make this holdup outright legal."

There was the rustling of silk cloth and the light footsteps of a woman. Johnny turned to see Mary Dark cross the floor to the bar. "Mr. Eccles, I understand you are interested in mining options."

Eccles took off his hat, and his muttonchop whiskers worked up and down as he talked. "Yes, Miss—"

"Dark. Mary Dark. A young man sent me these. He's dead now, and I wondered—"

Eccles looked over the various papers. "Yes, miss, my company would be interested in a number of these—especially this one, which should be worth, say, eight hundred dollars?"

"Eight hundred!" Mary's eyes shone.

"Yes, miss. Of course if the young man is now—ah, dead, these will have to be probated, but I think that can be easily expedited so as to save the full value of the options."

"I'd be very grateful," she said, "if you would take charge of them."

"Eccles," said Johnny, "don't you think that one option is worth a lot more than eight hundred dollars?"

Eccles threw his head back at a slant. "My dear young man, my business is dealing in mining properties. I assure you—"

"I heard you offer eight thousand dollars for that option," Johnny said, and walked closer and said under his breath, "and if you tell who the woman was I'll slice you up like a side of bacon." He was now on the opposite side from Duke, who was at the desk.

"Oh, yes," said Eccles quickly. "Yes, to be sure. Well, miss—" he turned to Mary—"I'll have my attorneys check. So much depends on the location, but as this young man suggests—"

Johnny nodded in approval. He thought he saw the pattern now. Mary was getting out from under, and perhaps would take her parents with her. Since Dark couldn't sell his business, this was a lucky windfall for him. But Johnny, watching all these friends of his getting pushed around, began to feel stubborn about it. He watched Mary leave, with no direct look at him, and then again he heard that gravelly voice:

"Options, Mr. Eccles?" Tallman took the papers from Eccles's hands. "Very good properties. I'm interested in options myself." He looked at Eccles and frowned. "How is it, Mr. Eccles, you can come into my town and pick up stuff like this when I didn't even know it was here?"

"Well, ah—I'm a businessman, Mr. Tallman. I—"

"A businessman, eh? Being a businessman, then you know what a partnership contract is. And you know what it means when two partners sign a contract that neither one can sell without the consent of the other?"

"Yes," said Eccles. "I know what that means."

"I've got a contract like that with Albert Dark," said Tallman, "and these options legally belong in his business!"

Tallman turned on him. "Where does a girl like her get options like these?"

Johnny opened his mouth but closed it again. Tallman had the options now, and he would keep them. That much was certain.

Chapter Nineteen

TALLMAN was nodding his head. "I'm a fair man, Mr. Eccles. I'll play you a hand of poker for these options."

"I don't seem to have any choice," said Eccles.

"Of course a two-handed game is not much fun." Tallman raked them all with his eyes. "So you, Johnny Concho, and you, Duke Lang, and you, Mr. Benson, will sit in. Mr. Eccles and I will play for a side bet; the winner will take the options. Otherwise it's just a regular game." He looked around. "You're a poker player, aren't you, Mr. Eccles?"

"Ah—yes."

"All right. Everybody sit down." He stood back and watched them sit down. Then he strode forward, tipped a chair back, and went in over the top without taking his eyes from them. "We'll play for money," said Tallman. "I don't like chips. I think all of you gents can afford fifty dollars. There'll be a five-dollar limit on bets—unless you want to raise it."

Johnny felt the tension rising within him.

"Too bad we can't wait for Helgeson and the judge and Albert Dark," said Tallman. "They'll be in later, I suppose. All right, deal, Johnny Concho!"

Johnny shuffled. Duke cut, and Johnny dealt.

Benson said, "I'll open for a dollar."

Eccles said, "As I understand it, Mr. Tallman, these options constitute a side pot which will go to the one of us who has the best hand."

"That's right."

"I take it that if one of us drops out, that will constitute a loss."

Tallman grinned. "You're a businessman, Eccles."

"And there will be only the one hand."

"That's right."

Eccles gathered up his cards and straightened them without looking at them. "I'm a man of curiosity, Mr. Tallman."

"All right. Start askin' questions."

"These options were in my possession. You have forced me to put them up as stakes."

"Yeah?"

"What are you risking against them, Mr. Tallman?"

Tallman's eyes narrowed. "You're too damn good a businessman, Eccles. This is my town, and I make up the rules to suit myself. You're in my town. You play by my rules— or you keep the hell out of my town!"

Eccles said finally, "I see," and picked up his cards.

Benson said, "I opened for a dollar."

"I will call," said Eccles.

"I'm in," Tallman growled.

Duke Lang pushed out a silver dollar, and so did Johnny.

"Cards?" said Johnny.

"I wish it to be known," stated Eccles, "that I am playing this game under protest."

"That's a good word," said Tallman. "I used that word once myself."

"Three cards," said Benson, obviously under a strain but trying to weather it.

Eccles looked at his hand. "I'll have two," he said with satisfaction.

Tallman looked at his cards and threw away one. Johnny dealt him one.

Duke Lang glanced at Johnny, then at Tallman, and finally at Eccles. He seemed to be debating with himself, but finally he shrugged and tossed out three cards. Johnny dealt him three.

Johnny looked at his own hand. He was one card shy of a diamond flush. He tossed one and took one.

"Bet," ordered Tallman.

"Five," said Benson.

Eccles raised it five. Tallman, without looking at his fifth card, raised five more. Lang called. Johnny called.

Benson shook his head and dropped out. Eccles called Tallman and raised five. Tallman, still without looking, raised five more. Lang called. Johnny looked at his cards. He had drawn a club. He dropped out.

Eccles said, "You want to raise the limit between you and me?"

Tallman grinned. "Make it a hundred if you want."

Eccles nodded. "Up a hundred."

Tallman said, "*And* a hundred."

Lang pushed the pot to one side except for the $300 just bet. "I'm in this one," he said, "but you gents can play with the big one."

Eccles said, "Up another hundred."

"*And* a hundred," said Tallman.

Eccles was sweating. He knew then he was beaten, no matter what he held or what he bet. "I call," he said.

Tallman picked up the fifth card and slid it into his hand, sliding off the two bottom cards and putting them on top, and going through this same motion again and again, keeping the men pinned down with his eyes while they waited. Then he laid them down one at a time, face up: the ace of clubs, the ace of hearts, the six of diamonds, the ace of spades, and the joker.

Johnny's eyes widened. Duke Lang had never allowed a joker in the house in his life.

Lang's eyebrows were raised too.

"I take it," Eccles said finally, "that you are using the joker."

"Aces, straights and flushes," said Tallman, and grinned broadly.

"You neglected to tell me that at the start," Eccles said coldly.

Tallman shrugged. "House rules. You know what a joker is, don't you?" He laid his hand on the options and closed his fingers, crunching the papers. He took the money and put it in his pocket. "Now," he said, "the house is buyin' a drink." He looked at Duke, and Duke said wearily, "Set 'em up, Harry."

Johnny got up and went to the door. Tallman's whiplash voice stopped him. "Johnny Concho!"

Johnny turned. "I'm here," he said.

"The house is buyin' a drink."

"I heard you," said Johnny, "but I'm not drinkin'."

"Johnny Concho, come back and drink!"

Johnny said quietly, "I'm not armed, Tallman, and I'm not drinking."

Tallman hesitated.

"And," said Johnny, "I'm not going after a gun, so you have no excuse to shoot me in the back."

Tallman said, "I'm going to get you, sonny. I told you once to get out of my town."

Johnny said, "I wouldn't live in your town, Mr. Tallman."

"Does that mean you're leavin'?"

"I've got some business here," said Johnny, "but I don't like to be pushed."

"Remember one thing, sonny: I get a cut of all business in this town."

"I'm remembering," Johnny said. He waited for a space, but Tallman turned away, and Johnny stepped outside.

He wondered for a moment if Red had been something like Tallman. It was an unpleasant thought, and yet that was the import of all he had heard.

If it was so, the Conchos owed a big debt to Arizona.

Johnny stopped by Judge Tyler's office. The justice, with his gold chain hanging across his vest, was deep in a Law Reporter. "Come in, Johnny," he said.

Johnny sat on the edge of a table piled high with books and scattered papers. "It wasn't a very good trade, was it?"

Tyler sighed. "It's utterly fantastic what a man can do with a six-shooter."

"None of this can be legal," said Johnny. "He's using his guns as a threat to make people sign things."

"Technically, yes—but the truth is that it may as well be legal unless someone has the courage to appeal to the courts."

"And you mean to tell me nobody has?"

"The one who does will get shot."

"But the town will be saved."

"That's not much consolation," said Tyler, "when you're dead."

"What is?" Johnny asked as he got up.

He went over to Bennie's for a cup of coffee.

"What's going to happen, Mr. Concho?" asked Bennie.

Johnny stirred his coffee. "It seems to be happening already."

"I vow I can't sweat it out much longer," said Bennie. "I'll just up and leave Cripple Creek. I homesteaded here. I married here. My wife is buried back up there in the hills, near the homestead, where she asked to be buried—so she could look out over land." Bennie's voice broke. "I—do you want sugar, Mr. Concho?"

"Don't mind if I do."

Eccles and Benson and Pearson came in. Eccles was wiping his brow. "That was the most outrageous thing I ever saw," he said. "That was robbery—just plain robbery."

Johnny stirred his coffee.

"Isn't that what you say, Mr. Concho?"

"It looked that way to me," said Johnny.

Eccles was sputtering. "I know he slipped that joker into his hand. It was new; it had never been used."

"You didn't point that out to him, Mr. Eccles," said Johnny.

"Would you have?" asked Eccles.

"I don't know for sure," Johnny said slowly.

"This is a preposterous situation," said Eccles.

"It's worse than that," Benson agreed. "It's humiliating."

"I got a question to ask, Mr. Eccles," said Johnny. "Is that one option really worth a lot of money?"

"To us it is," said Eccles, "because it throws a cloud on our title. To an individual it probably would not be worth very much."

"Then you would really pay eight thousand dollars to get that option from Tallman."

"We have no choice. We're operating a million-dollar concern."

"What if Tallman wants sixteen?"

Eccles shook his head. "I suppose we'll be held up, all right, but if it is within the range of possibility we'll have to pay it."

"What's their legal status?"

"They've been assigned to William Concho by a woman named—"

"That's enough," said Johnny. "So it doesn't actually make much difference whose hands they're in; the value is still to William Concho or his estate."

"Within limits," said Eccles. "We have a case here where the value may fluctuate rapidly, and I think the best procedure would be for the court to appoint an ad-

ministrator with power to transact business relative to the
options until the estate is settled. That way the full value
of the options may be realized at once."

"And who would be the administrator?"

"Someone suitable to the heirs, I presume—and to the
court."

Johnny tried his coffee. It was still hot. Pete Henderson came in, wheezing a little, and sat down.

"Terrible thing about Sam Green," he said.

"What are you goin' to do?" asked Bennie.

Henderson looked up, his hat pushed far back. His eyes
were troubled. "If we had a younger man for the job, I'd
turn over my badge." He sipped his coffee. "Trouble is,
I'm too old to fight and too young to die. I don't want
to die—and that's what facing Tallman means. The man's
a killer. He's got no mercy. I've faced many a man like
that—but that was twenty years ago."

Johnny was thoughtful. "Why was Tallman up at Silver
City today, do you suppose?"

Eccles spoke up. "We strongly suspect that he is con-
templating taking over the mines, the same as he has done
here in Cripple Creek."

"Why not the town?"

"The town is too big for him now—but let him get a
foothold in the mines, and he'll run the town in no time."

Joe Helgeson came in. "I'm thinking of closing my
blacksmith shop."

"Too much for you?" asked Henderson.

"It's too much for anybody. Today he tried to make
me play poker for the gold saddle."

"I take it you didn't," said Johnny.

"No. I would burn it first! I'll throw it on the forge
and burn it to a crisp."

Johnny said, "Bennie, what kind of pie you got?"

"Apple," said Bennie.

"All right," said Johnny. "Slide a hunk over this way."

"You want a fork?"

Johnny had just started to pick the pie up in his hands,
but he remembered Sam's wife telling him to use a fork
instead of a knife, and he thought about Sam Green's widow waiting for him to come home, and he knew what a
feeling of terror would go through her when she saw the

spring wagon coming slowly up the valley in the moonlight, and he said, "Yes, a fork."

"We got a lot of things to think about," said Henderson.

"That does not include me," said Eccles. "I'm getting out of this town as fast as I can."

"That won't be till morning," said Bennie. "Milo will come through about ten o'clock."

"That murderer may have my false teeth by then."

"Well," said Bennie, "what do we do next?"

Johnny got up and threw out a quarter. "I've got to go up to Mrs. Brown's," he said. "Whatever happens, I want my bills paid up."

Pete Henderson looked up, puzzled. "I kinda had the feeling, Johnny, that you was with us, that maybe you—"

"If we had somebody to speak up for us—" Helgeson said doubtfully.

Johnny turned on him sharply. "Sam Green spoke up, but none of the rest of you raised a finger."

Helgeson looked down at his coffee.

"It was the shock," said Bennie plaintively. "We never dreamed—"

"You better make up your mind," said Johnny, "if each one is going to be scared for himself or if you are going to act together like a town should." He stood up and looked at them. "You're all cowards," he said. "Every one of you—just as I was a coward." He paused to let it sink in. "It will take better than that to get rid of Tallman."

He left them sitting there and went to Mrs. Brown's.

"I want to settle up," he said.

"You owe me an even dollar."

He paid her.

"What are they going to do about that awful Mr. Tallman?" she wanted to know.

"That's a question," said Johnny. "He killed Sam Green tonight, you know."

"Sam Green! He was my first beau!"

"He's dead now," said Johnny. "Shot in the back."

Mrs. Brown sat down, holding her hands over her eyes. "Poor Mrs. Green! I will have to get up there. She will need some help!"

"That's a good idea, ma'am."

"I suppose she will bury him up on the hill on their place there, where they buried their second child. I wonder if he's got a hired man there who can dig a grave."

"I wouldn't worry about it," said Johnny. "Sam Green was respected in Cripple Creek. There'll be plenty to dig his grave."

"And the funeral! Who will preach the funeral? They didn't have a preacher for their baby, but—"

"Barney Clark," said Johnny. "That's his territory up in there. You inquire for him at Valley Center. That's where he lives."

"I'll send a message by Milo. And you, Johnny Concho, where are you going?"

He looked at her, not seeing her. "To the Copper Diggin's," he said finally. "I've got some things to say to Tallman."

She stared at him, her eyes filling with fright. "You haven't got a gun, Johnny."

"I know," he said. "I don't need one."

He turned and went out quietly and walked over to the general store. Albert Dark was sitting back in the corner.

"I really don't know what I'm going to do, Mr. Concho." He shook his head.

"We've *got* to face Tallman," Johnny said.

"Not at my age," said Albert Dark. "I'm not a young man any more; I'm old and tired and scared."

"Scared of his own shadow!" Sarah Dark said from the doorway. "Or he'd never have signed away this store."

Johnny sniffed the cheese and it smelled good, but he didn't touch it.

"That's all right," said Dark. "Help yourself, Johnny. I don't mind, really. It's just sort of between friends this way."

Johnny frowned. "You consider me a friend?"

"Yes; after you left and I got to thinking it over. You didn't cost me very much, Johnny, and you didn't really do anything very bad. After you left I got to thinking it was pleasant to have you come in here and help yourself to a piece of cheese."

"It was thievery!" said Mrs. Dark.

"No, now, Sarah, that isn't the same. When Tallman comes in for something it's like he's ready to kill anybody who opposes him; but when Johnny used to come in he was pleasant and he smiled and I didn't really mind."

Johnny sat down near the cheese. Dark got up and picked up the knife and cut a thick slice. He scooped a big handful of crackers out of the barrel and stacked them on top of the cheese and handed it to Johnny. "Try it, and see if age has improved it any," he suggested.

Johnny got crackers on both sides and crunched through them and into the cheese. He took a big mouthful and chewed it down. "Pretty good," he said finally, "but I think a couple of sweet pickles would help."

He went over and took the glass lid off of the pickle barrel and fished in it with the fork until he had four sweet pickles. He sliced the cheese through the middle and arranged the pickles between the halves. Then he tried it again. "One of the best cheese-and-cracker sandwiches I've ever set my teeth in," he said.

Sarah looked at him—maybe not as belligerently as she had before. She got up, listening. "I heard somethin' moving in the back yard," she said, and went out through the curtains.

Johnny examined the cheese for the next bite and said thoughtfully, "I know a nice piece of ground up north. I was aiming to buy it some day for Red and me, only I didn't know—"

"Didn't know what, Mr. Concho?"

Johnny got off of the counter. "I didn't know Red was a coward," he said.

Sarah ran in through the curtains, her eyes overbright. "Mary's gone!" she cried. "And she took the rifle!"

Chapter Twenty

JOHNNY stared at her. He stuffed the rest of the cheese and crackers in his mouth. Then he started for the door. Albert Dark stopped behind the counter to get his derby, and then came around the end of the counter to follow Johnny.

Johnny made for the saloon at a run. The place was crowded, but he didn't see Mary. Eccles, Pearson and Benson were at the bar, looking scared. Helgeson, Tyler, Bennie, Pete Henderson, and Mrs. Brown, along with at least thirty more, were in the room. They all looked grim. "What is it?" asked Johnny.

"Tallman is upstairs," said Henderson. "When he comes down—"

Johnny saw Albert Dark coming through the doors, his derby pushed back on his head. "When he comes down—what?" asked Johnny.

Pete Henderson took a deep breath. "Johnny, I'll fight him if you'll back me up."

Johnny started to answer, but he heard a sarcastic laugh in the rear of the crowd. Old Josh, the swamper, had come back to town. "Johnny fight!" He cackled. "Johnny Concho has been runnin' from a fight for a thousan' miles!" His voice was a little thick. "He come to Valley Center to get married, Mason and Lem from Rawhide got him cornered, and he denied his own name to save his hide. Denied his own name! If it hadn't been for the preacher, Johnny Concho would be lookin' at six feet of dirt right now—because Johnny Concho is yellow! He's a coward—a dirty, yellow, coward!"

"That's enough!" said Helgeson.

Johnny's hands were moist in the palms. He rubbed them on his pants.

Tallman was coming down the stairs, and Johnny heard the rusty hinges of the swinging doors. He looked back and saw Mary come in, and from the set look on her face he realized suddenly why she had given the options to Eccles: to keep them away from Tallman.

187

Tallman, in his black clothes, was now fully in the light, and Johnny pushed through the crowd to meet him. Tallman stopped at the bottom of the stairs, cold-eyed, and his gravelly voice said: "I told you to get out of town, Johnny Concho!"

"My memory is bad," said Johnny.

"I'm tellin' you once more."

"You're scum," said Johnny. "Scum that has to be cleaned out of Cripple Creek."

"Who's gonna do the cleanin'?"

"We are," said Johnny. "All of us."

Tallman snorted scornfully. "You ain't even packin' a gun!"

"I don't need one," said Johnny.

Tallman scowled. "I'll give you ten seconds to draw, Concho."

"I have nothing to draw," said Johnny, "but I'll get you anyway. This town is going to destroy you, Tallman."

Tallman's hand moved toward his hip. "I'm warnin' you for the last time, Concho. I've got a gun."

"Sure," said Johnny scornfully, "you've got a gun and you can kill me. Maybe you will. But the power isn't in the gun. It's in the people. You're through, Tallman, and no gunslinger will ever come in and buffalo this town again."

Tallman drew his gun and fired. Johnny felt it slam into his left shoulder and jerk him back off balance. Barney Clark hadn't told him how hard it was to die. Blackness poured over his brain, and he felt himself going to his knees. He heard Mary cry, "No! No!" Then the blackness passed and he was on his feet. "Try it again, Tallman," he said.

Tallman, obviously unsure, raised the muzzle of his gun. But a shot sounded from behind Johnny, and the pistol flew out of Tallman's hand. Johnny turned his head and saw Mary Dark lowering the rifle. Her father, with a .45 clutched tightly in both hands, shut his eyes and pulled the trigger. Tallman lurched. Walker came into sight from under the stairway, but Duke Lang stepped up behind him and dropped him with the butt end of a pistol at the back of Walker's head.

Tallman, swaying, snatched one of Walker's pistols and

fired at Dark. Pete Henderson took careful aim and pulled the trigger, and a hole appeared in Tallman's black shirt. Tallman tried to fire again, but his bullet hit the ceiling. Judge Tyler watched him until he raised the gun again, and shot him in the arm. Walker got to his feet and started for Tallman's side. Duke said, "Hold it!"

Walker snapped a shot at him. Duke fired, and Walker fell, hit between the eyes. Tyler shot again at Tallman, and the man went to his knees, but still he tried to level the gun on them. Albert Dark fired again, still clutching the pistol with both hands. He hit Tallman once more, and the man finally went down, his head falling on the second step of the stairs.

Johnny looked at Albert Dark. There was a glaze over Dark's eyes, as if he had been sleepwalking. "I did what you told me," he said to Johnny. "I held it with both hands."

Sarah walked up and gently took the smoking pistol from his hand.

Pete Henderson looked down at Tallman's body as he put his pistol back in its holster. "It looks like Cripple Creek has maybe come to its senses," he said soberly.

Duke said loudly, "The house is buying, folks."

Johnny went to the bar. Judge Tyler said, "Let me look at that arm."

"It's all right," said Johnny. "Nothing busted. It went on through."

Pete Henderson helped Tyler put a bandage on it. He said, "Johnny, I need a deputy. Cripple Creek isn't always going to be so little. With mining activity and all, I could use some help."

Johnny said, "Are you offerin' me a job?"

"Part-time, anyway."

Johnny took a drink. "You don't even know whether I intend to stay here or not."

"Sure you're stayin'," said Pete. "This is where you belong. You're one of us."

Joe Helgeson came in the door dragging a saddle by the horn. He looked happy and proud. "You'll need a good rig to ride up there to Sam Green's funeral tomorrow," he said. "I reckon this one'll fit you."

Johnny looked at the beautiful saddle and the gold filigree and he rubbed it with one finger; then he took off his bandanna and polished the smudge he had made. "Right nice saddle, Joe," he said. His lower lip was quivering.

Mary came up. "I'm glad you're staying, Johnny. I knew you'd be back. I knew it up there at the church."

She threw her arms around him, and Johnny blushed. "Right here in front of all these people," he said, "it ain't decent."

She put her lips against his. Suddenly everybody was looking the other way, and he held her hard against him.

Pete Henderson was standing on the bottom step of the stairway. "Folks," he said, "this here means the end of gun-rule in Cripple Creek. From now on I'm doin' my duty, knowin' that you're all behind me."

"We'll stand behind you," said Joe Helgeson.

"Me too," said Bennie.

Pete Henderson's eyes were misty. "It's a real good feelin'," he said.

Johnny smiled, and while they were still looking at Pete Henderson, he kissed Mary again. It was real good kissing, for her lips were like the petals of a mountain rose.

THE END
of a novel by
Noel Loomis

Noel M(iller) Loomis was born in Oklahoma Territory and retained all his life a strong Southwestern heritage. One of his grandfathers made the California Gold Rush in 1849 and another was in the Cherokee Strip land rush in 1893. He grew up in Oklahoma, New Mexico, Texas, and Wyoming, areas in the American West that would figure prominently in his Western stories. His parents operated an itinerant printing and newspaper business and, as a boy, he learned to set lead type by hand. Although he began contributing Western fiction to the magazine market in the late 1930s, it was with publication of his first novel, *Rim of the Caprock* (1952), that he truly came to prominence. This novel is set in Texas, the location of two other notable literary endeavors, *Tejas Country* (1953) and *The Twilighters* (1955). These novels evoke the harsh, even savage violence of an untamed land in a graphic manner that eschewed sharply the romanticism of fiction so characteristic of an earlier period in the literary history of the Western story. In these novels, as well as *West to the Sun* (1955), *Short Cut to Red River* (1958), and *Cheyenne War Cry* (1959), Loomis very precisely sets forth a precise time and place in frontier history and proceeds to capture the ambiance of the period in descriptions, in attitudes responding to the events of the day, and laconic dialogue that etches vivid characters set against these historical backgrounds. In the second edition of *Twentieth Century Western Writers* (1991), the observation is made that Loomis's work was "far ahead of its time. No other Western writer of the 1950s depicts so honestly the nature of the land and its people, and renders them so alive. Avoiding comment, he concentrates on the atmosphere of time and place. One experiences with him the smell of Indian camps and frontier trading posts, the breathtaking vision of the Caprock, the sudden terror of a surprise attack. Loomis, in his swift character sketches, his striking descriptions, his lithe effective style, brings that world to life before our eyes. In the field he chose, he has yet to be surpassed."